For Lebibe Rexhepi

NAOMI HAMILL

HOW TO BE A KOSOVAN BRIDE

SALT

LONDON

6528578.

PUBLISHED BY SALT PUBLISHING 2017

2 4 6 8 10 9 7 5 3 1

Copyright © Naomi Hamill 2017

First published in Great Britain in 2017 by
Salt Publishing Ltd
International House, 24 Holborn Viaduct, London EC1A 2BN United Kingdom

www.saltpublishing.com

Salt Publishing Limited Reg. No. 5293401

A CIP catalogue record for this book is available from the British Library

ISBN 978 1 78463 095 9 (Paperback edition)
ISBN 978 1 78463 096 6 (Electronic edition)

Typeset in Neacademia by Salt Publishing

Printed and bound in Great Britain by Clays Ltd, St Ives plc

Salt Publishing Limited is committed to responsible forest management.
This book is made from Forest Stewardship Council™ certified paper.

HOW TO BE A
KOSOVAN BRIDE

How to Be a Kosovan Bride

THEY WENT CRAZY for weddings after the war. All weekend long, the shooting of impotent bullets into the air, the aggravating honking of horns and the incessant drone of the traditional Albanian music. As if they were so glad to be alive that they wanted everyone from Podujevo to Pristina to Tirana to know about it. We are alive, we exist, we are marrying, we are playing our choice of music, we are wrapping ourselves in the fierce red of the Albanian flag, we are driving expensive cars that we didn't pay for and we are having babies and we are eating our turshi and carrying on our ways of living. *Perendi ke meshire per ne.*

Of course, it took a while before all this started. The confidence didn't come at first. At first they were like spiders, scurrying from house to house, the grey grain silo towering over them. But when they could walk from house to charred house, only looking over their shoulders once to see if they were being followed, they began to feel better. When the schools started back and the hospital opened and UN tanks were seen only once in a while, then they trusted that they might be okay. The war is over, thank God, *falenderoj zotin,* they would say. *Faleminderit Tony Blair,* our hero. *Faleminderit Bill Clinton,* the greatest leader America has ever seen. We are free. We will live. We will marry. We will move on.

It must be traditional, the fathers would say. A traditional wedding. An Albanian wedding. A wedding we can be proud of. We are survivors and we will live our lives.

So, the girl, for she was only seventeen at the most, perhaps sixteen or maybe fifteen, would be made to look twenty-seven, with the dark painting of the eyes flicking with drama at the ends and the bejewelled dress that clung to every part of her miniature frame, showing that she was a woman, she was ready. She must look modern. She must look expensive. She must look American, British, Albanian. No, she must look Kosovan.

But she must not smile. She is sad to be leaving her esteemed family. She cannot bear to be parted from them. She is full of sorrow for the respectable father and the loving mother she is forsaking. That is, if the mother and father have been left for her. Otherwise it will be an aunt or an uncle, arranging this marriage in place of them.

Of course, she is moving to another esteemed family. But for now she is full of the bitterness of parting. She will not raise a smile or rejoice in her humanity, still intact, though jeopardised by fighting. Not that she can remember much of that anyway. The frozen nights in the hills are just a far-off memory, or does she only even remember them because of the recitation of the stories by every adult in her family? Not every adult, of course.

No, she will stay serious and she will not smile. She will set herself apart, the portrait of the distressed woman, and play the part of the dutiful daughter of Albania.

But inside she is so happy, of course. A suitable man from a suitable family. A traditional family. A family with honour and dignity. An Albanian family. A Kosovan family.

She is the first of her class at school to be married. Whilst learning English in the overcrowded classroom with the scowling teacher who wishes the class would pronounce 'night' properly, she whispers to her friends about her engagement, the elaborate plans for the wedding, the aunts and uncles travelling from Germany, the glamour of it all. She knows that amongst her friends she is seen as special. The first bride. Married before she finishes high school. She'll have a husband and a lover. The girls giggle over the idea of a lover. She does not tell them that he has already begun to teach her what he wants from her. She cannot look at her hands as she remembers where he has asked her to put them. She supposes that this is part of the pathway to becoming a wife. And now she knows things that the other girls do not know, wifely things. Things never spoken of by anyone. And that is what every girl wants.

She chose him herself, of course. He is a friend of her older brother and he was at her school. He began to talk to her when he visited the house. Slowly, at first. Respectfully. And then he made her laugh and told her she was *bukur*, so beautiful. He sent teddies, dresses, sweets for her mother. He deals in the clichés of love. But she has been taught to expect these tokens, to expect these things and the new names: sweetheart, darling, *zemer*.

And his family, his father, come to talk to her family. Serious talk in the living room. She cannot be a part of this, but she knows that her father is defending her honour. She knows that he is making it clear that if this boy, this man in the making, does not honour his daughter and marry her now, now that he has shown a clear interest, that his family will find that boy and will hurt him so badly that his face will ache into the sweating summer and the unkind winter of the next year.

That his hands will bear the scars of betrayal for the rest of his life. And that, although he has slim chances of employment anyway, he will never ever find a job in this town, should he let her down. Her father smiles but he is not really smiling. And he lectures for a while, of his daughter and his family's honour. And he says that she is not to be left now. That they will marry, that he will not have his daughter rejected by other men, because she has been pursued by this one. This is all said in the loud and friendly tones of jovial conversation, over Russian tea and the stirring of the thick Turkish coffee. They are friends, their families know each other from old. This family rode in the tractor with his grandfather, deep into the precarious safety of the hills. But they both know that this all must be said. There will be no parts missing from the ritual, the contract, the tradition. And he means it, every word that's uttered.

At school she is special, the first. The teachers congratulate her, smile. She is a good girl, she is learning well. Able to do mathematics, she can speak English proficiently and her portraits of her classmates are pleasing. A good girl who deserves this happiness. Of course, there is one teacher who looks at her but does not dare to speak. She teaches her geography and when the girl answers a question in class, instead of responding to tell her if she is correct or not, the teacher stares sadly into her face. The others laugh and say that the teacher was always a little strange, but the girl doesn't join in the mocking. Inside, maybe she knows.

The wedding day is electric. All around her she sees women made to look like film stars, dresses clinging to every line of flesh, made with the most expensive, cheapest of fabrics. They are watermelon green and pink, the pale yellow of the abundant peppers in the market, the azure blue of the plastic buckets found outside every shop in the town. They are ready to go to the Oscars, ready to prove to the world that they are beautiful, elegant, modern women.

She sees an aunt with shoes that take her breath away. The hundreds of diamante pieces wink at her with excitement. The straight back of the heel. That heel is so proud and aloof. It is so glad to hold up this beautiful specimen of a woman, with her peroxide hair and the thick, theatrical arches over the eyes, revealing a daring that doesn't really exist. The woman knows that her shoes will cause excitement amongst the other women. They were sent by her brother in London and she tells them so. She is proud. She hopes that she might visit him one day, she says, although she, and the other women, know that the visa would never be allowed.

Still, they smile and they greet each other. The men with their sincere handshakes followed by the placing of the hand on the heart. We love our people, this placing is saying. We mean what we say. We are a people once more. We are honourable men. Of course, we do not talk about the browser histories in the internet cafes, or what happens in the woods, unreported, some days. We are honourable men. We will live our lives.

And the women. The women are preened to perfection. Some can hardly walk, others can hardly breathe, but they look astounding. They have taken all week to prepare for this wedding and the twinkle of the plastic jewels and the shine of the surprising dresses and the Albanian red of the lips, ready to kiss each other in greeting, show that it has been worth it. It is a wedding. We will look glorious.

As the music begins, the women take to the floor. There is

no need to think, as the *one, two, three and back* of the dancing that they learned when they were just girls comes as naturally to them as walking. Their faces hide any sense of excitement or embarrassment or joy or sadness. They will remain blank, their eyes staring, glazed, as their legs take over. The women hold their hands, linked, into the air, each forming a bridge that, unlike Gredelica, will not be broken. We are a nation, they are saying. This is how we dance and we can carry on all night. There is no need to think. This is part of who we are. The woman on the end waves a small handkerchief, but there is no energy lost in this action. It is as though the rhythmic movement of her arm is as much a part of her as the chopping up of the peppers, or the mixing together of the flour for the flija, or the steady weaving of the intricate yarns into jackets and tablecloths, or the carrying of her child into the mountains to some sort of nervous safety. The line of women travel the floor, each connected, each showing that she is now a proud mother of Kosovo, a sister, a daughter, a wife, a friend.

She has never seen anywhere as beautiful as this. It was paid for by the shacat, the sweetie pies, as they affectionately liked to call them. Those who got out during the war and now were so rich that they could send back money from Germany and could arrive for the summer in their Mercedes and drive them boastfully round the town. They must be so wonderfully happy, those shacat, she thought. And so kind. She was so grateful to her uncle for paying for her wedding without question. She did not know that this whole wedding was pitifully cheap by German standards.

This wedding must be spectacular. Of course, they all know that after the wedding, when she is a wife, there will be scrimping of euros and turning off the generator if the salary isn't paid, and the grateful relief at the gift from Germany each month. But for now, they will shine.

The music fills the place. The enticing mix of Eastern and European sounds. It leads the dancers on, through the evening and around the room, entrancing them all. The men will join in later and will show their honour by their enthusiastic flinging and flicking. They will swivel their arms in defiance and scoop their legs from one side to the other in careless abandon. It will get noisier and the children will melt to the sides, sleeping on golden hotel chairs. The women will pick at crisps and drink Fanta. The men, outside, will smoke their cigarettes. The music will continue. They will dance for the entire evening. They will live their lives.

The Kosovan bride will remain in her chair. Although she is not smiling, they all know that this is the most glorious day of her life. Later, when they are ready to leave, they will pin notes to her and kiss her and wish her love and blessings from God. Her face will stay emotionless, of course. She is a good girl and she will show respect to her family.

The Kosovan bride will not be found by her older cousin in the toilets of the expensive hotel, so expensive that she has never seen such luxurious handwash before, locked away and stubbornly trying not to cry. She will not be afraid of what will come next. She will not insist that she cannot, will not, let this man, this disgusting boy, touch her again.

All this will not happen. You will not let it.

How to Pass a Virginity Test

WHEN THE WEDDING is over, when the aunts and uncles and neighbours and cousins have pinned more euros to her dress than she has ever seen, the men begin to pull up the cars and taxi these glamorous women back to their villages and their farms, back to their unfinished houses and their generators, back to their cleaning and their cooking and their own wedding videos, which they will watch over and over and over, remembering their day of greatness, their slim waists, their sombre faces, their last goodbyes, their peanuts and their Fanta and their turn to belong at the hotel for just one evening.

One car may break down by the side of the road and one woman will stand in the pitch black, at the edge of a road full of speeding cars and trundling tractors, tired but brightened by the excitement of the evening. In her finery and her carefully painted face, she will tell her husband how much she loves weddings and how much she wants him to hurry up so that she can upload all her photos to Facebook that very evening, so that her aunts in Hamburg and her sisters in Stockholm and Manchester can see the wedding and can comment on the pictures of the dresses and can feel at home, even though they are so far away. She wants her sisters to see that, although she is one who stayed, she can still sparkle and gleam and pout and impress, for one evening, at least.

The Kosovan bride did not sob until her mascara tears

dripped onto your shirt. She will not have cried into your crisp, white shoulder and told you that she is scared and that she has changed her mind. She will not have bowed her head and looked at you with the most serious face you have even seen. She did not ask you so earnestly to fix it for her, like you have fixed everything so many times before. You will not have seen in her teenage face both the buoyant little girl she was ten years ago and the woman with a softening of jaw that she will become in another twenty. Your heart will not have fluttered at this sight and entertained her request for just one second. Your eyes will not have blinked back a whisper of water. Your voice will not have shaken in an undetectable way when you told her that it is a matter of honour and dignity and that she is a woman now and that all will be well. You will not have doubted yourself at all as you said these words and stroked her hands and told her that she made an oath. You will not have felt a little ashamed when you emphasised the dishonour a reversal would bring on the family and when you told her stories of women who did not choose their husbands, who were not treated to such luxury, such sophistication. You will not have looked away when you told her to remember how lucky she was to have such beautiful heeled shoes and reminded her of how excited she was when she first became engaged. You will not have told her to remember the teddies and the love notes and the secret little smiles. None of this has happened.

And you did not ask a cousin to wipe her face and re-apply her garish lipstick. You did not raise your voice when she gave a final little sob. You did not tell her to grow up and to do what is dutiful and right and honourable and correct. You did not walk away from her and give her five more minutes to do what she should. You did not tell her that if she did not go home with her husband's family this very evening, then no desirable man would want her again, that she would never have any children. You did not say these things.

The Kosovan bride walks to the car that her husband's family have borrowed from an uncle who is over for the summer from Germany. How respectful of her to retain that sorrowful look, even this late into the evening, her new mother-in-law thinks. How dutiful and honourable this girl is. What an excellent choice my son has made. She is a traditional girl and she respects the customs of our people. Still, it is late now and she does not need to look this way for long. The girl's mother has gone home early with a headache and the girl can relax, smile, maybe even look a little pleased, her new mother-in law says to herself. There are no one's feelings to protect now, she thinks.

The Kosovan bride sits in the back of the car with her husband. Outside, her father and her siblings wave at her, with shouts and laughter and gun shots flying into the air. She sees a lurid scene before her which looks like something from the television set in their front room. The stiff uncles with their buttons undone, her father, never emotional, giving a vigorous handshake to her new father-in-law. The men, smoking outside the building, the waiters going home for the night in their casual clothes, her new mother-in-law and sisters-in-law twinkling for the final time in the darkness and then slipping away into cars and taxis, back to their home, her husband's home, her home from now on.

She is the only woman left at the wedding.

As a cousin drives them away she feels her husband's hand move under the layer of her skirt and up between her shaking thighs. 'Don't be scared,' he whispers in her ear, 'this is what a husband does.'

She hears his smugness and the determination in his voice and she tries to tell him, 'Not here, not now, just wait, just wait.' There is a shrillness to her voice that irritates him and he stops trying to be tender, gentle.

'Wait,' she says, again. 'Just wait. Please.'

But the Kosovan groom is tired of waiting. Three times he has tried this before and she has always spoken of honour and dignity and he has waited, because that is what his father expects and what his mother would want. He has put up with the occasional pleasures and the reservation of her body, because he understands how his people work and he wants to be able to expect the same from his own sons. Not that he hasn't done this before, with a girl in the city at a rent-by-the-hour hotel and another from a bar, a few months ago, just for relief. Not that he's waited for this. But he's waited for her, his wife. And tonight he will wait no more.

By the time they reach the house he is holding her by the arm. 'You're hurting me,' she says, as he takes her into the house. And he keeps a grip on her as he says goodnight to relative after relative and kisses his mother in the hallway. He keeps hold of her arm as his mother kisses her softly on the cheek and praises her for her respectful, honourable attitude. 'What a wonderful girl, what a good girl, what a wonderful wife for our son, a true Kosovan bride,' she is saying. 'Not like these girls in bars or these cousins in London with their tattoos; a traditional girl, a respectful girl, that is what we wanted for our son, and that is exactly what we got,' she is saying, tears in her eyes, pride in her fierce Albanian heart.

The Kosovan bride asks him to let go. 'I'm sorry,' he says,

but there's something in his voice that she didn't detect nearly a year ago and she talks to him of the way he was, with the teddies and the messages. 'I really wanted to marry you then,' she says, and she tries to call him sweetheart, to make him remember, but he doesn't even look her way and he is almost pulling her along the hallway now. Her face is red as his older brother laughs at his eagerness, out of earshot of the traditional parents, of course.

And she says she must go to the bathroom. And she locks herself in and she sits on the side of the bath whilst the tiles and the sink gleam at her and whilst the smell of disinfectant and shampoo fill her nose and whilst the hem of her wedding dress soaks up water from the floor and she notices the brown marks at the bottom of her very special, once-in-a-lifetime dress, the most expensive dress she will ever wear. She thinks of her mother sewing on the tiny little plastic pearls and of her father paying for it with money he has been saving. And she hears his calls to come out through the door and she does not answer. She does not even lift her head to look that way.

And then his mother is sent for and he explains to his mother that he is worried she is ill. The mother coaxes out this little creature and dries her tears and tells her that they were all scared once but that she will become a woman tonight and that she will be a proud Kosovan mother one day and that her dress will clean and that her son will look after her forever now. She makes him sound like a dove, a lamb, but the girl knows better, the girl knows better. *I know better*, she thinks but does not say. Cannot say. Will not say. Must not say.

She walks to the bedroom to join him and remembers that there is nothing to be done. She darkens her heart and keeps on breathing. *You will survive*, she tells herself. We are a strong nation, we will live our lives. There is nothing that does not make us stronger.

The Kosovan bride. A startled rabbit in a trap.

And you, you do not think of her, as you snore in your bed, full of food and full of family and full of doing your duty. You lie there, splayed out on your sheets, inert, snoring into the night.

The respected men of the house, his father, his uncles, a few cousins, his older brother from Germany, wait up into the night, long after the wedding is over, their cigarette smoke and their talk of their language twisting together into the air and dissipating like vapour into the night. They argue over words, which one fits the sentence better, which one is the correct one to use in such and such a context or such and such a poem. Sometimes the older brother Googles a word on his phone and finds something to back up what he says. 'The internet cannot be trusted,' says the father, 'but our ancient texts, they are to be trusted.' They all agree that this is true. 'Words matter,' they say. 'Our words matter,' they say. 'Our words have survived,' they say, 'and we are sure that they matter.'

Then later, when all the women are in bed and just the father and an uncle and the brother still remain, the Kosovan groom joins them for a cigarette. 'And of course she did,' he says, in answer to their question. They shoot bullets into the air and the father lectures, long and powerfully, about the honour of this evening, this day, this marriage, and he says that it is right that it should be like this. 'Just as our forefathers,' he says. 'Just as our tradition,' he says. And he touches the domed white hat on his head and tells them a story from Albania. 'For our people died for us,' he says. 'Our red hearts bled for this,' he says. 'Blood is necessary sometimes.'

How to Fail a Virginity Test

T HERE IS A knock at another father's door at four in the morning. This father makes his way to the door and stands there, barefooted, whilst a man he has shared Russian tea and stories with just a few hours ago says that he must take his daughter back.

His pale little daughter, another little Kosovan bride, wrapped in a blanket cocoon, stands between him and this man, shivering.

'There was no blood,' he says. 'No blood, no tradition, no honour,' he says.

The long seats that line the walls of the house, just as they would have lined the walls of the kulla years ago, are now the setting for an hour-long conversation. The seats are velvet and green and swirl with pattern; too ornate for this kind of conversation, too ornate for this. And his wife fetches tea, and his wife fetches socks for her husband and the daughter. And his wife keeps breathing in and out, despite what she hears, despite what she wants to say, despite what she knows, deep in her heart.

The silver teapot is kept warm and the small glasses are kept full of tea. The tea is poured and the words are poured. The words are scalding, hot, liquid, poured out of angry, hot mouths. Accusations are made. Accusations are refuted. There is talk of honour, oaths, respect. And what of our honour, oaths, respect? Aren't we entitled to that too?

These conversations are loud and long. There is much to-ing and fro-ing, this way and that way. The girl says she has not, she does not know why, she has never. And the father does much sighing and frowning and he makes stern faces and speaks deeply to this man. And the father-in-law gestures with his hands and talks of honour, tradition, honour, tradition, honour, tradition, honour, tradition and blood.

'There must be blood,' he says, 'there must always be blood.'

And, in the end, they agree that she will be returned. There will be no more arguments or anger or continued discussion. There will be no more bargains and pleas and questioning and accusations. She will return, along with her wedding dress and her suitcase. She will return, along with her fear and her tears and her little shaking hands.

You did not wake up for this. They thought that your anger and your heart would shake up the house with this. And they didn't know which way it would turn. They didn't know if you would rage at her or at them, so they left you to sleep, unaware, in your bed, of the transaction and the conversation and the anguish and the returning.

The Returned Girl makes her way back to her own bed, the second she has been in this night. This one is smaller, neater, squarer, plainer, safer. She opens her own drawers and takes out her own nightdress. She lies on her own pillow and she thinks her own thoughts. And the darkness creeps in. And the shock creeps in. And the anger creeps in, is kept down, is kept low.

And her body will remember this night. And her mind will remember this night. And her eyes will remember this night. And her lips will forget this night and her mouth will not speak of this night and her tongue will never utter this night.

And the Returned Girl keeps breathing in and out, despite what she heard, despite what she wants to say, despite what she knows, deep in her heart.

Her little toes are frozen, wrapped in her blanket, so late into the night and the morning now. Like little frozen seeds, buried, deep in the ground, unsure of their precarious future.

How to Be a Kosovan Wife

O F C O U R S E , T H E girl who becomes the Kosovan Wife
does not need to be taught anything about cooking and
cleaning and looking after the house. She knows how to reach
deep into every crevice and wipe out crumbs, so that the mice
will stay out and so that ants will keep away. She knows how
to sweep every square centimetre of the kitchen. She knows
how to chop up the brightest of red tomatoes and the greenest
courgettes. She can mix and stir and taste and season. She can
mend and sew and make and fix.

And she has other skills too. She teaches her mother-in-
law how to send an e-mail. She gives her father-in-law the
injections that the doctor left. She is not just a traditional girl,
a domestic girl, a respectful girl, but she is a modern girl, an
e-mailing girl, a Facebooking girl, a clever girl. She has made
herself useful. She has made herself liked. She has made herself
part of the family. She has made herself indispensable.

When the older brother returns to Germany, she sets up
Skype on the laptop for her in-laws and they gasp with happiness when they see their grandson on the screen. 'You are
a magician,' they say, 'you are a wonder and a delight and
we can never repay you for what you have done.' For three
days her mother-in-law makes her favourite food for dinner
and breakfast and she strokes her hand and pinches her side
and kisses her cheek when she can. The mother-in-law keeps
returning to the screen to check that the icon has not gone

away. 'I do not want to lose this gift; will my grandson still appear tomorrow?'

'What a clever girl you are,' they say. 'What a wonderful addition to our family. So good, so respectful, so traditional, so hardworking, so loyal, so good with computers.'

'What a clever boy you are,' they say, 'to have picked such a wife. And imagine the children you will have. Imagine the children.'

The newlyweds have come to some sort of a truce. Now that he is over the initial desire, he looks at her in a different way and sees that there are many years ahead. Last week he bought her some perfume from the market and it meant something to her. It really did. And she, in turn, tries to hide her lack of enthusiasm for his less-than-gentle advances and she spends an evening trying to find out about Manchester United, his favourite football team, so that they have something, anything to talk about.

And nowadays there is only night time when they are alone together. She spends all day with his mother and his aunt and his cousins and their babies. And on some special days her own mother and her own sister join them and they watch wedding videos and listen to music and she paints her nails in pink, red, orange, blue, silver, purple, yellow. And there is the cooking to be done. And there is the cleaning to be done. 'And one day soon she will have a child too,' they say. 'And one day soon she will have a child too,' they hope. 'And one day soon she will have a child too,' they nag.

The Kosovan Wife isn't sure about this. She's still getting used to her own gangly body. She isn't sure she wants another swirling inside just yet.

Her husband's sister has a job. She wears nice clothes and

works in the court and is respected by many people. *I've finished school*, she thinks, *I could get a job too.*

'But there are so few jobs,' they say, 'where will you get one? Leave them for the men. We have enough and you will have a baby soon, we're sure.' *But the sister has a job*, she thinks. *Why not me? Why not me too?*

Late at night, she Googles YouTube channels with free English lessons. She tries to learn an extra ten words a day and dreams of her teachers, her school. One night she dreams she is flying over the town on a magic carpet, speaking English to everyone and they cheer her and applaud her and no-one makes her cry.

How Not to Be a Kosovan Wife

'AN OLDER MAN, a widower, it will have to be,' the father of the Returned Girl says. He spends a day telephoning relatives and e-mailing his list of contacts. He writes a list in a scrawling, busy hand and she stands silently by his side in the living room while he makes the calls. 'There will be someone,' he says. 'There will be someone.'

He is gentle with her, kind. He believes her. 'After all,' he says, 'I have always protected you from men. From the violent ones when you were a child and from the dishonourable ones when you were older.'

'I have heard of these cases before,' he says.

'Not to worry, little chick,' he says. 'There will be someone. God has a way of working these things out.'

You, usually the first to be strong and bold, do not interfere. You feel you did quite enough and secretly, at night, you stare wide-eyed at the ceiling and wonder at the decision you made to make her honour her oath. *She has not been honoured in this*, you think. You know she is an honourable girl, just maybe a little too soft, too butter-like for the world. You remember playing together, when she was a little girl and you were only a little bit older, walking into the hills with her holding your hand and singing a traditional song about a virgin and a snake.

He's beginning to go bald and is getting to be that kind of fat that shows a move from youth to age. 'Not him, not him,' the Returned Girl insists, when her father shows her a picture. 'Please, Father. Not him.'

And then another, a man in the market who sells parts for washing machines. 'His wife died in childbirth,' her father says. He has a little girl but he's only twenty-two. He has a pointed nose and kindly eyes and the Returned Girl thinks he may not be so bad.

'But isn't there another way, Father?' she says. 'Can't we put it off, at least for now? I am doing well at school and I could try to go to university. I could marry after that, surely? Isn't this another way? Lots of girls in the city do this.'

And now you get involved and you undo what you did. You've seen the way the teachers talk about her at school. You've seen their eyes that say she is a clever girl. You've heard the jealousy in the other girls' voices. You've seen her work displayed in the classrooms. 'Let her try, Father,' you say. 'She has tried the other way and it did not work. Let her try.'

So, it is decided. Each night, after dinner, the table is cleared for the Returned Girl, and her mother gets rid of all the crumbs, scooping them neatly into her hand, and she spreads out an embroidered tablecloth she made herself, when she was just the Returned Girl's age. And the Returned Girl piles up her books and she does extra work. She goes through the photocopied English textbook and learns every piece of vocabulary in the glossary at the back. She jumps ahead of the class and does all the exercises until the end of the book. And for mathematics she asks the teacher to set her extra work and then she uses the internet to look up what the students in England are learning at her age. She works through each question, each sum, each piece of work with a look of steel. With a mind of steel.

At school, some of the boys make comments as she walks past. They say that she was returned, not wanted, used and worthless. She does not flinch, does not falter, does not even say a word. She knows that actions are more powerful than words. She has had a taste of a narrow escape and now she is working for no more narrow escapes, for no escaping at all.

In the hills, her family has had a taste of narrow escapes and they want no more narrow escapes, no escaping at all.

A shy boy, one who hides his hands in his pockets and shows his ideas with his quietness, smiles at her and says that he thinks that she is brave. The kindness makes her heart grateful, but it will not happen again, she will not mistake that feeling for freedom again. No. She thanks him and then stays away. As quiet as the boy may be, she knows the consequences of shy smiles and gentle looks. She has had a taste of a narrow escape and now she is working for no more narrow escapes, for no escaping at all.

How to Be a Kosovan Mother

TOO LATE. THE rounded stomach.

'Just like a watermelon,' her mother-in-law says.

'Just like my wife,' her father-in-law says.

Her husband does not comment. At least it seems to put him off.

She walks the swollen walk to the clinic, with her mother. 'Not long now,' they say. She wants it all to be over. The heat of the summer is beginning and she wants it all to be over. She does not recognise her body; she does not think that it was meant for this. The clinic is full of pregnant women and their mothers, sometimes headscarfed, sometimes peroxide blonde. There's chatter about the latest scanning machine and someone says that their daughter in Germany managed to get a 3D scan. 'Whatever next!' they say. 'Perhaps that will be us one day, if God allows.'

'In England,' another says, 'the father is usually in the room when the woman gives birth.'

'How strange,' another says. 'What use would a man be for that kind of thing?'

Of course, it is natural. It is hard to think that a mother will not love her child. And she does love him. She finds his smile intoxicating. And his recognition of her face is more precious than gold. The birth was not as bad as she was told it would be. After all, she is young. After all, she is not even twenty yet.

She wraps him in blankets and cradles him and looks with longing at his hair, his nose, his little flaky fingernails, his chubby little legs, the soft down covering him like a peach.

When she manages sleep, her dreams are full of those nights in the mountains, when she was just a little girl. Only she isn't the girl and her mother isn't the one holding her hand. The Kosovan Wife is the one holding a little boy's hand. And she is willing him through the woods, and she wipes the snotty little nose and they tramp through the never-ending mud together, always being pursued. Sometimes her feet get stuck in the mud and she is sinking and sinking and trying to hold the little boy above her head. Sometimes she is in the woods and she hears gun shots all around. She lays him down and crouches over his small body. She always wakes with a racing heart.

The Kosovan Wife's days have become his days now. Feeding, dressing, washing, playing. It's not that she is bored, it's not that she is bored. And there are so many people to hold him, to pass him round like a little basket and to kiss him and to fill him full of love.

Her husband likes his son. He wraps him in an Albanian flag and photographs him on his phone. One day he places a toy gun by his side and something in her wants to tear it away before the photograph can be taken. Of course, she laughs like everyone else and says, 'Yes, yes, he will be brave and a fighter. Yes, yes, of course, our nation breeds strong, valiant men who will never be struck down.'

Inside, she prays for peace for him. *May he never have to hold a gun*, she prays. *May he never have to see a friend killed in war. May he never know what it is like to flee for your life.*

Alone with her baby at night, feeding him, she whispers

old Albanian folk tales as she rocks and soothes. But never those which talk of war. Instead, she whispers words of love deliberately into his ear: *peace*, she coos; *kindness*, she sings; *gentleness*, she murmurs; *reconciliation*, she prays.

How to Pass a Kosovan Exam

TO GET TO university in Pristina, the Returned Girl must pass the national exam of Kosovo. It examines all subjects: Albanian, English, mathematics, science, geography, history. She cannot be good at one subject and bad at the rest; she must excel in them all. Which is fine, as she is generally good at learning. But if, say, she had a flair for English and an impeccable accent, but could not do algebra to save her life, well, then, she could not enter university to study, even if she wanted to study English and travel to London, that most beautiful and desirable of places. She would not be able to fulfil her heart's desire because she must pass the national exam. It is an inconvenience at least, a filthy road block that could ruin her life at most.

The teachers in Kosovo, and the parents, and the students, all believe that this is unfair. Why should anyone who is good at some particular subject not be able to study it at university?

The directors of the schools and the teachers have come up with the most ingenious of plans. 'Who will ever inspect our examinations?' they say. 'Who will know what happens? And what we are going to do is a kindness, a blessing to our future generations. And the generations of the past have suffered enough,' they say. 'Why curse the future?'

So, on the day of the national exam in Kosovo, those students who are very good at English will have studied their English notes very fastidiously. Those students who have a natural talent for mathematics will have brushed up their quadratic equation skills to the limit. Those students who can name every river in the Balkans, all in the name of geography, they will have learnt all there is to know about the natural world. Everyone will have studied hard. But if you have a specialism, you know that today is your chance to shine.

The students will gather in big halls to take the exams. They will sit at a desk and would never dream of bringing in cheat notes or looking over someone else's shoulder so that they can pass. No, that would never happen.

They will all scribble away, eager to secure their place in Pristina University, their only ticket to the outside world. They know many of the answers. They have studied hard, after all.

About half an hour into the exam, when everyone has made a valiant attempt at the first section, the teacher will ask a boy to stand. This boy is, by far, the most able mathematician in the school.

'Read out your answers to section one,' the teacher will instruct.

Faithfully, the boy reads out his answers and his fellow students write them down. This boy does not mind – he is glad to share – he knows that he is helping out his classmates and he feels proud of his achievement.

'*Faleminderit.* You may sit down.'

Section two is very hard this year. It covers aspects of the Albanian language that are complicated, even for the teacher.

Another twenty minutes pass and a girl is asked to stand. She does not need instruction as she mechanically repeats what is written on her page.

And so it goes on, subject by subject, until the examination is complete.

At the end of the exam the pupils are congratulated: 'Well done. You have been a good class this year and you have achieved much.' They are all warm with pleasure; they know that they have worked hard and the teacher, not often one to compliment, has recognised their desire to learn.

You may be shocked to hear these methods. You may think that they are unfair and do not constitute a proper exam.

Consider this:

- Say you are an eighteen-year-old student, with good marks, all earned yourself, and you apply to university. You may be rejected because another pupil's aunt works for the police.
- Say you are a 'morning shift' student, so are only allowed to attend school between 7am and 1pm. Your class size is 55. The English teacher cannot be there for the morning sessions.
- Say you cannot go to school every day because you must care for your father. He does not have a whole arm.
- Say your father cannot afford a notebook for you because he has no relatives living in London or Germany.
- Say you are a girl and your destiny is marriage. It seems pointless to study because you will soon be making bread.
- Say you are dyslexic, but no-one has heard of dyslexia in your village. It is not even dreamed of.
- Say that, born in America, you would be a brilliant architect, but art lessons in your village school are limited to painting portraits.
- Say you have a stutter and cannot speak out in class.

- Say you are a fantastic tennis player but you have never held a tennis racquet.
- Say your mother left your father (an extremely unusual and shocking occurrence) and you can no longer see her; it is all you can think of. It makes you sick just to think about what might have happened to her. This makes study impossible.
- Say you know that the whole police and political system is corrupt and jobs are granted based on political allegiance.
- Say your people were considered worthless enough to wipe out.

I am sure you will now agree that these Kosovan directors and teachers are life's geniuses. They are the kindest people you will ever hear of. They are full of humanity and love these children more than any smiling, creative teacher in England might be able to, even though their faces are stern and their sentences formal.

The thing about the Returned Girl is that she doesn't need any of this. The Returned Girl is going to get the best marks in the school. The Returned Girl wants to go to university more than anything else she can think of. When she washes in the morning, the desire is there. When she pours the mixture for the flija, the desire is there. When she cleans her teeth at night, next to her older brother, the desire is there.

She will pass the Kosovan exam, for sure. And she will apply to university.

How to Build a Kosovan House

THEY ARE GOING to build a house. A house for all the family, with three layers and a cow in the garden, attached to a very long rope, of course. There will be chickens roaming free outside the house and it will be made from bricks of the brightest orange. There will be fruit trees surrounding the house and they will build a long drive so that, when the family visit in the summer, a long line of cars can snake down this impressively long driveway. There will be balconies and large, shining garage doors and gleaming windows and a brick wall to protect the garden.

The Kosovan husband has been working in town. He sells mobile phones on the streets in the evenings and in the day he builds for the municipality buildings department. Which is how he can get the materials cheap. Which is how he can get his friends to come and help.

They already had the piece of land. On the edge of the town, they had a house there before the war. 'Before the devils came and burned it down,' his father says.

'Before they stole our gold and broke our hearts,' his mother says.

And they have lived in a cousin's house all these years since then. But with the money his father has saved and with the money from the brother in Germany and with the help and connections he has fostered, they can build. They can build! They can build! Thank God! *Falenderoj zotin!*

'We are going to be so happy,' they say, 'returned to our own house, our own land, our own honour. When we are entertaining guests, we will be able to tell them how this house came to be. We will talk of my grandfather buying this piece of land and of the sense of peace we feel now that we are back in our rightful place. Let those snakes see that they could not destroy us. Though they killed my mother and they made us run for our lives, let them see that we will never be kept down. We are strong, we are Albanian, we are builders, we are Kosovan. Oppression can never keep us down!'

So, after work and at weekends, they begin to build. They use some of the old house and its base and build on top. The Kosovan husband says that he is building for his son. 'One day, he will bring his own wife here and this will be his house,' the Kosovan husband says. 'One day, I will be an old man with a white hat on my head and I will play chess all day long and I will live with my son and I will be proud, for I built him this house.'

The Kosovan Wife is caught up in the happiness. The Kosovan husband has a purpose and he is even kind, some-times. *When we will live in this house*, she thinks, *I will never be afraid. When we will live in this house, he will never make demands. When we will live in this house, everything will be better. Our own home. Our own place to bring up our children.*

Children, because there is already another on the way.

Each day, in the late afternoon, they go to the land and build. With scaffold made of large branches, they begin the work on their new home. Brick by brick, hour by hour in the scorching heat that does not break, even into the evening.

The Kosovan Wife goes too. She takes burek for the men and large bottles of water. She takes her little boy and they find the edges of the land, picking peaches and apples as they wander. The little boy is beginning to walk and he takes his first steps on the place where they will build. *How appropriate,* she thinks, *what a sign of a good future!* She kisses the boy's shining cheeks and films his wobbling steps on her phone.

How to Have a Kosovan Dream

THE RETURNED GIRL is eighteen and bold and bright. Always in competition to get the best marks in her class. There are three of them who fight for this position, but more often than not, it is her.

She's particularly good at English. Even though there are forty-five in her class, and there aren't enough seats and so usually she can't sit down, it is her favourite lesson and she loves learning all about the simple perfect and the past perfect simple and the proper nouns and the modal verbs. But mostly, she likes the photocopied textbook with the pictures of Big Ben and the Tower of London and she dreams, at night, of going on the tube and getting lost in all the twisting colourful lines of the tube map. The colours wrap her up so safely, the lines excitedly spin her round. She vows that, one day, if she ever gets to London, she will ride every tube line from top to bottom, from left to right, from corner to corner, until she has been everywhere. She does not understand why everyone in London does not do this.

Each Saturday, when helping her father load his car with peppers for the market, she wears her favourite T-shirt. It is emblazoned with a British flag and she was given it by a neighbour's daughter, when it got too small for her. 'Our cousins in Britain sent it, last year at Bajram,' the neighbour tells her proudly. She also uses Saturdays for speaking English with her friends, on the phone, or in the town, or via Facebook. She checks herself into places in London on Facebook and she and her friends 'like' these places and write comments underneath, as if this is how they have really spent their weekends. When they meet at school on Monday morning they discuss their weekend in London. As if this is where they have really been. As if this is what has really happened.

The girl is hardly ever cross, but if her mother has not washed this T-shirt for each Saturday, she stamps around the house and slams the doors. 'It is my British day,' she tells her. 'My one day when I am happy. My one day when I am free.'

Secretly, her mother worries. At night she whispers to her husband that she thinks the girl has too much imagination and that maybe they should sit her down and tell her about the visas again. The husband shares her worries but he gently says that he thinks that they should let the girl have ambitions and hopes. 'One day, she may get there,' he says, 'we do not know the future. What it is for us may not be what it is for her.'

The mother does not say this, but this is not her worry. Inside she fears that the girl is only dreaming of heaven and she anticipates her heartbreak when she will discover that it is not London, it is not Britain. She prays she will not get there, because she knows that it will only break her heart.

How to Make a Kosovan Cake

THE BEST DAY of the year. Bajram. Cake day! Visit upon visit to houses where plates of cakes are served. Little nutty chocolate cakes, sponges with banana through the middle, bouncy little coconut-speckled mouthfuls. Tiny forks, little plates, Fanta and Coke and tea. Handshakes and smiles and stories and family and chatting.

The Kosovan Wife has been baking all week. If the visitors come and there are not home-made cakes, what will they say? They will say that this is not a good home. They will say that this household has no pride. A Kosovan Wife will never serve shop-bought cakes. It is impossible to think that this will happen.

Which is why she must stir in the coconut-flakes. Which is why she must mix up the sponge and watch the oven. Which is why, as her bloated stomach weighs her to the chair, she will still get up and mix the butter in, although her mother-in-law says that she should just sit down. 'I will do it,' she says, 'I will make the cakes.' But no. The Kosovan wife wants to do it herself. Remember, she was once a very good student. Now she wants to be a very good wife.

Relatives come and go. There are waves of neighbours and each is given a plate of cakes, a glass of Coke, a tiny fork, a hearty welcome. They sit in the garden today, on plastic garden furniture, in the shade, and listen to crows cawing overhead. She remembers an English lesson in school where they learnt collective nouns. A pride of lions, a herd of elephants, a gaggle of geese, a flock of sheep, a murder of crows. That's right, a murder of crows.

Her little boy is running around. He has eaten so much cake today and the sugar is making him wild with excitement. The Kosovan husband gives him a glass of Coke and she protests: 'There's too much sugar in that,' she says, 'he's already acting crazy.' The Kosovan husband ignores her and gives the boy the drink.

When her mother and father and sister and brother arrive for cake it is towards the end of the day. They bring gifts for the little boy: chocolate, a teddy bear, a tiny Kosovan football kit, a toy gun. The Kosovan Wife puts the plastic gun away and thanks them for the wonderful gifts. She serves them cake and Turkish coffee. She runs her tongue over the gritty coffee granules and savours the sweetness of the taste. It is thick and delicious.

They bring her gifts too: a blanket for the expected baby; a new apron made of a thin yellow fabric, with green pears printed on top; some wooden serving spoons. 'For your new house,' they say.

'Thank you. Thank you so much,' she says.

Her sister puts her arms around her and cradles her tummy. 'You are getting fat,' she says, smoothing over the bump. 'Think about how skinny you used to be! Think about how small we had to make that wedding dress!'

They sit in a haze of cigarette smoke and listen to the sounds of the street. There are children running up and down, lighting firecrackers and squealing when they explode. The Kosovan Wife remembers when she was just a child and how these mini-explosions were the highlight of her year. Dogs bark at the loud banging as the explosives hurtle down the street. 'We will soon be away from these children playing out,' her father-in-law says. 'We will soon move to our family land, with our repaired house.' Her father asks him how it is going and he says, 'Yes, my son is doing us proud. The first layer will be finished before long and then they can move there and get settled whilst we sort out the money for the second layer.'

'Wonderful! Wonderful! How wonderful to return to your family's land,' the Kosovan Wife's mother says, 'and how wonderful for our daughter to live with you there.'

The Kosovan Wife feels a sort of sadness in her stomach. She will miss the sound of the children in the neighbourhood, she will miss being just three streets away from her mother, she will miss this garden and spending Bajram out here in the sun. Her mother-in-law has told her that women feel more emotional during pregnancy, but she thinks that this may be a separate thing. She feels a sort of longing for the past.

When they say that it is time to go and they all walk to the entrance of the garden to say goodbye to their visitors, like any respectable Albanian family would, she kisses her mother and holds on to her hand just a second longer than she might have done. Soon, there are tears and her mother kisses her cheek and says that she will feel better when the baby comes. They all laugh and talk of pregnant women and their feelings. 'Always very sad or very happy. I remember when my wife was pregnant,' her father-in-law says.

'She's emotional,' says the Kosovan husband.

'You'll feel better soon,' says her sister.

'Cheer up, sweetheart,' says her father.

Only you notice a deep sadness in her eyes. Only you wonder if maybe there is more. Only you think about her as you all walk home through the darkening streets.

How to Attend a Kosovan University

THE ABSOLUTE TOP of her school. The best marks anyone has received this year. She is proud. And she hears that they still call her the Returned Girl, even more so now, now that she has defied them, but she does not care. Suddenly the Returned Girl does not call herself the Returned Girl any longer. She begins to call herself new names: *clever, destined, free, hopeful.* She begins to whisper, *the university student* to herself, in moments of daring.

The night of the results, they eat in the local restaurant. There are bowls of peppers in cream, salty and delicious. There is bread, rounded and puffed up, like her father's chest tonight. There are salads full of bold red tomatoes and solid, pungent cheese. And there is meat, slabs of meat, and plenty of it. 'Bring us the best,' her father says, as loudly as he can, 'because my girl is the best in her school. The best marks in the national test: can you believe it? She did better than everyone in the whole school, better than all the girls and better than all the boys.'

'I am the proudest father in the whole of Albania,' he says, wrapping his arms around the Returned Girl.

'My girl will be a doctor, a lawyer, a teacher, the president of Kosovo,' he says. 'My girl. My clever, little, bold, hardworking girl.'

'You have made me so proud tonight,' he says, draping the red flag with the black eagle around her shoulders.

'You have made our nation proud tonight,' he says. 'It was for this that we did it.'

'Move forward proudly from the past, no matter what happens to you, that is what we Kosovans do,' he says, looking at his wife and sharing a moment of recollection.

You are proud too. She may be younger than you and you may not have done as well at school, but you are proud of her too. You do not say this to her, it is not your way, but you give her forty euros, money you were saving for your own wedding, and you tell her to go to the shops and to buy herself what she wants, a treat. You tell her that she has brought honour to the family and you are glad that it worked out like this. She looks at you with her wise little eyes but she does not reproach you about the past. She does not say a word.

Later, at home, after the excited chatter has died down and after her father has recited her marks over to himself for the last time, laughing and thanking God, the Returned Girl sips her tea and looks at her mother. She remembers the walking for days, but she remembers little else. She knows that you know more, that you were older and that you can remember, but she knows that you will not say a thing. So, she asks her mother about those days. 'Why do you ask me today, little chick?' her mother says. 'Today is a day to be happy, to celebrate the future, not look to the past,' her mother says.

'But, Mother, you always say you do not want to talk about it,' she says, 'you always put me off. I want to understand.'

'Focus on your future,' her mother says. 'Don't focus on the past.'

'But I want to be fully grateful,' she says. 'I want to fully understand what this means.'

'Focus on the future,' her mother says again.

So, university beckons. She has the best marks, no-one can argue with that, and she is given a place. What else could they do? No-one can argue with the best marks. She will study English. She wears her T-shirt with the British flag on it all day and at night dreams of tea cups, red buses, tube lines, Big Ben.

Her best friend from school hasn't been so lucky. She was tenth in the year. Still excellent. Still with university-worthy marks. They turned her away. But the boy down the road, who was twentieth, he still got in. She rages for her friend, asks her father to do something. 'Perhaps he has a relative who works at the university,' the father says. 'Or perhaps his father has a connection with someone,' he says. 'There is nothing I can do. She can work for a year and then re-apply. Or, if her family is rich, she can go to the American University.'

That day, the Returned Girl makes herself a secret promise.

How to Upset a Kosovan Family or How Not to Have a Kosovan Baby

AFTER THE BABY is born, they will move into the newly finished house. Just the four of them. *Like an American family*, she thinks. And when they have saved enough for the next layer of the house, then her father-in-law and mother-in-law will move in. And her husband's sister, until she is married in the spring. 'When the top layer is built, we will have space for twenty children,' the Kosovan husband jokes. She hopes he is joking.

They are packing up their belongings when the pangs begin. 'Let's not go too early to the hospital,' she says. She is folding up clothes and she is deciding which pots and pans they will need. 'No hurry,' she says. 'I will be okay. Remember how easy it was last time?'

And it is easy. It is so easy and fast that they do not make it to the hospital and they have to run to a neighbour who works as a midwife and their little girl is delivered in their bedroom, right there in the house. 'Just like before the war,' her mother-in-law says, whilst clearing up the mess. She changes the sheets on the bed for the Kosovan Wife and she swaddles the little girl in a blanket. She coos to the little girl and jokes about her coming into the world too quickly, too precariously, too dangerously.

'You should have gone to hospital sooner,' the Kosovan

husband scolds. 'We have hospitals for a reason,' he says. 'We don't need to have babies in the hills like they did in the war,' he chides. 'Our parents saved us from this kind of situation,' he admonishes. But he is softened. By the newborn skin and the smell of a daughter all his own. He softens with the protective role he is now beginning to try on.

The Kosovan Wife does not lift her eyes. She does not look at him or even raise her head. She does not eat any of the food they bring her or drink any of the tea. Her arms feel too heavy to lift. Her head feels too solid to move.

'It is not natural,' she hears her husband saying, 'for a woman to ignore her child.'

'It is not natural,' she hears her sister-in-law saying, 'to stay in bed so long.'

Her mother-in-law calls for her mother. Surely that will make her better? 'Come on, sweetheart,' her mother says, 'you have things to do, you must get up. You have a baby and a little boy and a husband to look after. And a new house. Just think, a new house to move to.'

The Kosovan Wife feels like a stone. Her world is grey and not worth the effort. She cannot get her legs to move, she cannot get her arms to cradle, she cannot get her mind to think. The fog, the fog of cigarettes, but in her mind.

Her mother calls for the doctor. 'I have seen these cases before,' he says. 'What should be most natural for a woman becomes unnatural. What should be most normal for a new mother becomes a chore.'

'Plenty of rest,' he says. 'Plenty of rest and quiet and she will come round. There are drugs, but give it a week. You'll have to collect them from Pristina, if you need them.'

A week passes with no change. They try to whisper, they

45

care for the baby, they do the best they can. Even the Kosovan husband Googles the name the doctor gave it: *post-natal depression*. He lists the symptoms and lays the baby next to her. 'She has to bond with the baby,' he says. He tries not to sound angry when the Kosovan Wife turns away.

The Kosovan husband drives to Pristina. He collects the drugs and they seem to make it better. The Kosovan Wife begins to move around the house like a ghost. She sometimes lifts the baby. The baby's little smiles sometimes even make her smile.

How to Be a Kosovan
University Student

S HE SOMETIMES STAYS with her aunt in Pristina, the
capital city, in the week. She loves the bustling capital city.
Police with serious faces and long, black guns; women, arm
in arm, carrying the latest fashions from the most desirable
shops; a few foreigners (she could tell they were foreigners
straight away); men in shirts and ties, more men in shirts
and ties, more men in shirts and ties; babies being carried,
babies sat on laps in backs of cars, babies being cared for by
their siblings; children, at every window, every corner, every
street.

Buildings with the smartness of EULEX money, buildings
with the glamour of big brand money, hotels with grandeur,
hotels with lost grandeur, hotels with grandeur still to come.
Endless shoe shops with shoes displayed on shoe boxes, piled
into precarious towers; a perfume shop selling fragrances
emulating all the designer smells; a fake McDonald's; kebab
shops, burger bars, row upon row of coffee shops with low
tables lining every street; men smoking at every opportunity;
winding, half hidden streets that give her the urge to go and
discover what is at the end; buildings that look as if they
will fall into the road if she shouts too loudly; teenagers,
young people, trendy, dark, effortless, everywhere. And the
gorgeous cathedral. And the universities: the quiet, run-down,

47

home-run campus; the American school with the flashy sign and the smart young recruiters in the street. The university library with that dark, defensive look that makes her think that they really must love knowledge, to wrap it up in such a menacing manner, as if no one, just no one, is going to take it away.

Of course, she must always stay at home at weekends, as most people do, but in the week she joins a gang of students who stay with relatives in the capital, or who themselves have family there, and these are her most treasured days.

Of course, she has lectures and of, course, she is working hard. It goes without saying. For this is the Returned Girl and she has learnt to work hard to get what she wants and she has been rewarded.

And the reward has been this city and the freedom of living like this. She loves meeting everyone on her course. She is so happy to finally meet someone else who dreams one day of travelling on the London tube. She and her new friends sit in coffee shops and speak English. 'The best way to learn,' says the lecturer, 'is to watch English television, is to talk English as much as you can and to read anything you can get in the English language.' The Returned Girl is reading *The Hunger Games*. She was given it by an aunt's friend, when her daughter had finished with it, and she is transfixed. She almost cannot do anything else, because she does not want to stop. She has never felt this before. She thinks that if she could get access to English books, she would never do anything else but lock herself away and read. How do the writers know how to say exactly what she is feeling? How can they put it in those words, in exactly the right way?

And she loves the freedom of the coffee shops and bars

in Pristina, without her neighbours and aunts and cousins looking to see what she is doing. She sits with boys and girls in bars and no one will report it to her father. She can talk to anyone she likes and they will not remind her that her name is the Returned Girl. She sips at coffees and they taste of a new life. She talks at length with classmates about politics. Some of them have joined the youth party, Vetëvendosje! She isn't brave enough for this, but she snaps each of their graffitied signs with her phone and makes their slogans her Facebook cover photos. She loves their brave acts of rebellion and their passion for making their own decisions. Soon she might join, she thinks, but she doesn't want to let down her father, who thinks that the PDK is better, safer, more stable.

Mainly, it is what people are wearing in Pristina that she likes. There is an air of modernity around the town which seems like a confidence no one in her own town seems to have. The people wear clothes that are different; they walk with a sense of entitlement. *In my town*, she thinks, *everyone is so grateful.* Here, she notices, they feel it is their right to be alive, their right to belong. There are men in brighter shirts and sunglasses, off to business meetings. There are women who have bought their clothes in European chain stores. There are internationals and they look as if they are glad to be here. Not forced into a war zone or just feeling sorry for them: they actually look as if they enjoy living here.

Her favourite place to stand is the newborn statue. It is chunky and bold and has just been painted with the flags of all the countries that have recognised Kosovo as a country. She has had her picture taken there so many times, enjoying being part of the youngest country in the world. She has also been there, alone, in the late afternoon, when most of the onlookers have moved away and she sits, curled up, in the middle of the giant O. It feels to her like she is being cradled, a baby again. Just a newborn herself.

How to Move into a Kosovan House

S HE IS NOT the same, but she is walking and talking and picking them up and eating and sometimes sleeping through the night. 'It's usually babies who can't sleep through the night,' her mother-in-law jokes. 'You've swapped roles with your daughter.' She finds it hard to smile at this joke. She finds it hard to smile when the house is ready. She finds it hard to smile when they have moved in.

She arranges the kitchen, placing pans in cupboards and the tiny hourglass qaj glasses on a top shelf, away from the children. She holds her daughter at an angle, on her hip, whilst she cooks their first meal in the new house. She stuffs peppers with spices and meat. She covers them in oil. She adds a little cheese.

Her husband tries, just now, to be kind. He says that the peppers smell delicious. He says they taste of heaven. To her they smell of nothing. To her, they taste of nothing at all. Each mouthful tastes of darkness, nothing, darkness, but she cooks, she eats, she lives, she goes through the motions of each day.

The kitchen is so modern, with doors that lift and a breakfast bar. In the living room they have thick windows with blinds and a large black sofa that looks so new, so large, so imposing. There is a washing machine and a brand-new cooker with many different functions. Her in-laws are so proud of this home. 'It is our old, family home but with all the newest appliances,' they say. The best of both worlds: family and forward thinking; ancient walls and plastic surfaces; land we own with a house we have built up; memories of survival with hope for a better future.

The Kosovan Wife tries so hard to be grateful. She tries so hard to feel all that she should feel. She says that the enormous television they have bought them is the best she has ever seen. She forces herself to smile when she watches all the latest television shows. And when her husband goes out in the evening, she supposes she is grateful for the background noise, the company, the distraction.

'Look what I have created for us,' says her husband. She does say thank you. She does appreciate the fact that he has done this. She does know that others don't have what she has.

He begins to want her once again. Her insomniac nights are sometimes intermingled with a turning away so that he can feel relief. He does not seem to care if she is there or not, she thinks. All the movies she watches on her brand new television don't show sex like this. *Is that just a lie, or is this just a lie?* she thinks.

She does not want another child. It is one thing she actually feels in her endless days of feeling nothing. She tries to tell him but he does not understand. 'But we have a house now,' he says. 'I have a job now,' he says. 'My parents expect there to be more now,' he says.

She knows that she can see the doctor, but she knows to go to a local clinic is not safe. She knows that people talk. She knows that she will have to go to Pristina to make this happen. It is the one thing she is sure of and so she makes some plans.

Too late again. There she is with the test and a sinking feeling and a numbness in her hands. Again? She thinks she may lie down and never wake up. She cries most days. 'Just the pregnancy. You are emotional again,' says her husband. 'But, just think, we have another on the way, a new house, everything to look forward to. Nothing to be sad about.'

He has begun to stay out late a few nights. When she gets a little fatter round the stomach is always the time that he leaves her alone and always the time when he begins to stay out later. She supposes she should investigate. She can't even be bothered to try. She is grateful that someone else is dealing with what she doesn't care to deal with.

How to Ask a Kosovan Question

SHE ASKS AGAIN, her mother, about the past. But her mother gives the same response and the Returned Girl cannot ask over and over, she feels.

But she wants to know. She has flashes of memories and she knows the awful stories everyone knows and she's heard what people say. But she wants to know from their lips. It is part of her, even if she was only small.

Her lecturer has given her a task: to write a story in English. She tells them to write a story that means something. She tells them to write a story that is true.

The Returned Girl tries her aunt. Perhaps she will tell her some truth.

Her aunt asks her what her mother has said, when she has asked her to do this. The Returned Girl tells her that her mother cannot, will not, cannot talk. 'Too early, perhaps, too much, perhaps, too painful perhaps,' the Returned Girl says. 'But you. You could talk. Maybe it is the right time for you?'

She uses the voice recorder on her phone and they sit for three hours. The Returned Girl can barely breathe when she listens to the recording. She saves the file in twenty places so that it cannot be lost. She uses her aunt's words to write her story.

A Small Death

I F I TELL you my story, you must not cry. You must not shed a tear, wipe away a whisper of water from your eye, allow even a hint of moisture to build.

This is my story and it must be listened to in my way. I was strong. I didn't break, didn't shatter, didn't weep. You mustn't either. We must all remain as iron. If we don't remain strong, who will be left?

When they took our kind out of the hospitals, the women began to whisper. Women have babies, that cannot be stopped, it is the way of it, but where could we go? Would we be able to enter the buildings any more, even when birth had started, or would they even stop us from that?

And then we heard the stories. Women left to bleed. Women left to scream. Women left to rip. Women left to die.

And the babies: sick, hungry, hurt, stolen, dead.

I wasn't going to take a chance. A naive neighbour said that it could all be made up, that the rumours could even have been spread by them, to keep us away. But who will risk a child, a thimble-hearted baby, with a fragile heartbeat and those imploring eyes?

So, when it was time, we had a plan. There were women, older women, who had done it before, especially in the days before women could always travel to hospitals. They said they would come and that all would be well. He wasn't my first. We believed we could do it. Many women do, all over the world. Why should we be any different?

We prepared towels and water and all the painkillers we could muster. An old man who lived at the end of the town walked a mile to bring me the painkillers he had been saving, should things turn out as we all feared. 'For you, to help, with love,' he said. He smiled a wrinkled smile, 'I know your father.'

'*Shumë faleminderit*,' I said as I looked sincerely into those kind old eyes.

Our oldest was sent to fetch them. When the waves and shakes said it was time. When I winced and held my breath and leaned forward with pain. Then the women came. And they came with food and with teas and with blankets and with baby clothes. They came with advice and with love and with experience and with truth. It was a party of a sort and I was the honoured guest.

Yes, I was scared. Yes, I was anxious. Yes, it was violent and aggressive, like any new thing that will change your life and twist your heart like a cloth. But these women brought comfort. They helped me to deliver him with a special measure of triumph.

When he was finally born and gave his first cry, one woman held him aloft, my blood staining her shirt and forearms, and we all cried and wept and smiled and there was joy in that room. Pure joy.

'Despite you. Despite the fact that you hate us and want to kill our children,' she called out to the menacing leaders we had never seen and who may or may not have existed.

She passed him to me and a woman whispered into my ear, so close, the warmth of her breath felt like it was breathing new life into my aching body, 'As my own son, as joyful as my own son. We are all his mothers now.'

He was red and wrinkled and blood-stained from the battle of birth, but he had clear eyes and a strong stare and he was in my arms and we had done it. *Thank God, thank God, he is here.* I touched his arms, soft as ripe aubergines. I touched his toes, tiny as peas. His face glowed.

And then they cleaned and they cooked and they cooed over my other little ones. My husband was able to keep the garden going; we needed it for food. And this flutter of women spent two days gently cooking and softening us up in the butter of their hearts.

Our daughter cried when they left. 'Don't worry little one, we'll be back to visit your brother in a month or so, and when we come, we'll make sure there's a little something for you.'

We were all so grateful. We lived in a polished world of hope. We felt as we had not felt since the occupation, for at least a few days. We remembered the ordinary things that made us happy as the children played with the dog and helped my husband with the tomatoes. And although the fear and reality crept back in over the next few days, we had him, and it made our days shine for a short while.

Twelve days later he died. He had swallowed fluid during the birth and we hadn't known. What could we have done anyway?

It wasn't just my grief that rang out that day. We shared it and we shared his tiny body as we passed it around before giving him to the earth.

That same woman, the one who had whispered so gently into my ear moments after the birth, spat at a policeman on the way back from the burial, so I'm told, and he beat her until her face turned blue. 'Better off dead than living with this plague,' she screamed as he kicked her and kicked her and the others tried to drag her away.

How to Tell a Kosovan Story

T HE KOSOVAN WIFE is beginning to feel small things again. Like getting the feeling back in your toes when they are numb. And bed time is when she feels this tingling the most.

She has always loved listening to stories herself and, remember, she was very good at Albanian in school. Her grandfather would tell her tales and it would make her insides shudder just to hear those words, just to imagine those characters, just to live in her mind for a while. The stories would make her excited and nervous, all at the same time. These stories help her to remember; they help her to forget.

She thinks it is important to pass these stories on to her children. So, every night, she curls up with her little boy and her baby girl and the one who is beginning to swim around inside her (yes, another) and tells them many tales and fables and stories and poems and myths. She wants them to be able to tell these stories to their children. She wants them to take them into the future. She whispers of the mountains and the seas and the mysterious lands in which the characters live. She booms out the voices of the heroes and the villains. She entices them with delicious descriptions of battles lost and won.

But there is one story that she cannot forget from her childhood. She knows that she begged her grandfather for this story many, many times and he, in love with his granddaughter as all grandparents are, did as she wanted and told it over and over until it swirled around her mind and the words became her words, until the story became her story, until she was the storyteller herself.

The Maiden in the Box

THERE WAS ONCE a woman who lived in a small, dingy room in a dark house. She had hardly anything: only the clothes she was wearing and a small, wooden table and a tiny cot for her small son. Beneath the dirt on her face and the grime in her fingernails and the sorrow in her heart, this woman was beautiful, but the cares of the years and the worries of being so very poor had made her back stoop over and wrinkles had begun to grow around her eyes.

The son grew up to be very weak. This is hardly surprising because he was never given very much to eat and the room that they lived in was dark and damp and his blanket had many holes in it.

As the son grew up to become a young man, his mother said to him that he would have to go out and look for work. 'I am no longer able to feed you and you need more than I can give.' Although the young man wanted to work, he knew that because he was so feeble he wouldn't be able to get a job carrying things or moving things or doing any other job that the young men in the town did.

He told his mother that he didn't think he would be able to earn money but that he did have an idea. 'Remember my Godfather?' he said. 'He is a merchant and may give me a job. Then I will be able to earn money and send it back to you.'

So, they wrote a letter to his Godfather, with hope and trepidation in their hearts, and they posted it to him straight away.

How to Enter a Kosovan Competition

'**I** HAVE ENTERED your story into a competition,' her lecturer tells her.

The girl is flattered, honoured, pleased. She goes home to tell her aunt who is less pleased and wants her to withdraw it. 'Someone might know that it is me,' she says.

'Yes, that's right,' says the girl. 'And then they will know about your story. Which is important, which is valuable, which is worth telling.'

The aunt thinks about it over dinner and decides that it will be okay. 'But you didn't mention my name, did you?' she says.

The girl thinks about the competition all week. Imagine if she won it. The prize is one hundred euros and it will be published in a magazine. She will find out in three weeks' time.

For three weeks she wakes in the morning and the competition is on her mind. It takes over her thoughts of the London tube and her dream of Britain and it dances at the back of her throat for the whole time. On the day of the result she checks her e-mails twenty times. Nothing, no response, nothing.

She does not win.

How silly of me, she thinks, *to have expected to win a competition. How stupid, how arrogant, how completely ridiculous. Why would I win, when it is just my first story?*

Her lecturer is disappointed. She says that it is a fine story, a truthful story, one that should really be told. 'Keep writing,' she says. 'Tell the stories,' she says.

The Returned Girl does not stop listening. The Returned Girl does not stop writing.

School Before the War

HIS MOTHER TOLD him that he would be going to school at his uncle's house from now on. He liked his old school and he said so, but mother was tense and said that things would just have to change and that he could still like school at Uncle's house.

'But Uncle is not a teacher.'

'Uncle knows many things. He was very old before you were even born. You have a lot to learn and he has much to teach. Now go and pack your bag for school.'

It was a Wednesday and the next day they walked to Uncle's house for the first lessons. Strange, there were only fifteen of them, not the usual forty or so and some of their friends were not there, but it wasn't mentioned by anyone and he did not like to ask why, as it seemed that no-one wanted to tell him anything he felt he really needed to know.

Uncle seemed like a very ancient man. His thick moustache and eyebrows were all you really saw when you looked at his face and his skin was riddled with small red lines, as if his correction pen had escaped at night and decided to decorate him. He had a small brown dog that sat with him at all times and did whatever Uncle told it to do.

They gathered round in Uncle's front room, with Uncle in his wedding suit. The seats that they had sat on when they celebrated Bajram last autumn were now their chairs and they leaned on thick school books to complete their work, instead of having tables. There were no desks and no classrooms and no director to check on them.

'Will Director Rexhepi be visiting us today?'

'Not today.'

When they were allowed to play, three at a time, in Uncle's garden, skidding amongst the marrows and peppers and tomatoes, he asked his friend why this was all happening.

'Didn't you mother tell you? It's because of our language. Stupid boy, *jo shumë bayat*, don't you know anything?'

He knew that things were different. He knew that you didn't see the old men with their white caps in the town square playing draughts any more. He knew that on market day the chicken and rabbit sellers shouted in a hushed kind of way. He knew that mother's eyes had more lines around them. He knew that some children had stopped coming to school, but why?

Just a few months ago, if one of the neighbours' cows had misadventured into their field, they would shoo it back with a friendly wave and a *mirëdita*. Now, Father had built a fence at the bottom of their garden and they didn't see the neighbours at all.

It was a few days later, at Uncle's, that things became more alarming. They were just in the middle of learning about a way of subtracting long numbers from each other when they heard a knock on the door. Uncle placed his pen slowly down on the wooden coffee table he used as a desk and seemed to hold his breath.

'What's wrong, Uncle?'

'Nothing. You just keep working on those numbers. Do all that I have shown you.'

First they heard Auntie scream. Then soldiers came through

66

the door to the living room. They stared at each of them with disgust and one spat on Uncle's floor.

'Are you teaching these children?' they asked in a language they all understood, but which didn't come naturally to their mouths.

'I am,' Uncle replied simply.

A soldier took Uncle to the sink.

'Wash your hands.'

Uncle obediently took the soap, turned on the taps and began to wash his hands. When he had finished, he reached for a towel to dry them.

'You're still dirty, wash them again.'

Uncle, calmly, repeated the action.

'Again. I can still see dirt.'

Uncle obeyed.

'Again.'

The children stared in disbelief. Uncle's hands were clean and he should tell them so. But they knew better than to speak.

Thirty-six times Uncle washed his hands, until the edges of his nails were sore and pink.

'I think my hands are clean now.'

'Go outside.'

The soldiers followed Uncle as he walked to the garden, followed by his faithful dog.

Uncle returned, ten minutes later, his arms covered in soil and his face caked in dirt. He returned companionless.

'Don't tell us you are clean!' one soldier shouted at Uncle, right up close to his face. Then one said something quietly to the other, and they left quickly.

'We'll be back, so make sure you're clean next time.'

Uncle, with dirt stuck to his moustache and with his wedding suit ruined by soil, returned to his chair in the middle of the room.

He picked up his pen from the coffee table and carried on with the instructions for subtracting. The children, too frightened to speak, took lessons from this brave, muddy man.

How to Lose a Kosovan Baby

SHE IS WALKING the edge of the land with her children. Her little boy and her little wobbling girl, who has just learnt to totter around on her own. They have planted roses near to the house but out here, near the edge of the land, wild flowers grow and she loves the light blue ones, picking them for their table and encouraging her children to do the same.

Her little boy has learnt the word for flowers and he says it over and over, 'Lule, lule, lule.'

She's so very tired this morning. She keeps waking in the night with those terrible dreams, only this time she's got her three children with her and one keeps running off and she can't figure out which one. When the gunfire starts she's running around trying to gather them together. She always wakes with a racing heart.

Her little girl has fallen over again and as she stoops to pick her up, she feels a pain and then the liquid. She sits right down on the ground and lets the blood soak into the earth. The children are distracted, picking flowers and she whispers: 'May God accept you into his arms, little Lule.' She knows that it is over. She knows that it is finished.

Funny, to mourn a child you didn't really want. Funny, to have the mixture of relief and sorrow whirling in your brain. Funny, to think about it as a child when you thought before that it was a burden.

She lays some flowers over the place and walks back to

the house. Her husband says that she must see a doctor. 'You don't know that it is dead,' he says. But she knows. But she knows. But she knows.

She sees a doctor anyway. While she is there she thinks about asking for something to stop another pregnancy. But does she need to replace this one? Did she cause its death by not wanting it very much? If she'd held on to it tighter, would it have stayed?

She feels she has a duty to mother another child in its place. When he begins, a few weeks later, to clamber on top of her and part her legs, she doesn't resist or tell him about the pain. As she lies there in the darkness, she says sorry in her mind to her unborn child. *It was my fault*, she says. *I didn't love you enough*, she says. *If only I had cared a little more*, she says.

She lies in the darkness, when it is all over, wide-eyed and full of fear. She thinks about her father, and about when she was just a little girl and would wake with nightmares, and about how he would scoop her up and tell her tales to stop her feeling afraid.

The Maiden in the Box

'WONDERFUL NEWS!' THE woman told her son. 'Your Godfather is going to employ you. He says that you must go there as soon as you can.'

Of course, the woman was putting on a bit of a show about the news in the letter. She was, of course, very upset that her son would be moving away from her. After all, he was her only joy in life, but she wanted him to have a better future and they had to eat. Everyone has to eat, no matter how sad they feel.

So, she and her son began to pack his few meagre possessions into a bag. They did this very slowly and seriously, for neither of them really wanted this to happen. Then they walked to the port very slowly and seriously, for neither of them really wanted to say goodbye.

The boy put his arms around his mother. He didn't know when he would see her again, so he held on to her for a long while. He took a deep breath and walked away from her. He boarded the boat and promised to send all the money that he could.

'Goodbye, my darling boy,' his mother called as she watched him getting smaller and smaller and as she watched the boat disappear out to sea.

How to Spend a Kosovan Evening

S HE HANGS OUT in a hidden-away bar on Friday evenings. Always the same one, with her friends, before she
takes the bus back to her town on Saturday morning. They like
this bar as it plays low music, usually a woman singing along to
a guitar, and there are small lights outside, twinkling into the
night, and little candles on the tables. They often drink coffee,
and sometimes a little wine or beer, but she always feels guilty
about this the next day. She doesn't want to upset her father.

The bar is tucked into a little street beside Mother Teresa
Avenue. Sometimes, on the way back in the evening, they sit
by her statue and bask in her care.

Tonight, her friend has brought some friends. Three girls
and a guy, all internationals, all working for UNMIK. The
two girls are American, there is one British girl and the guy is
British too. She really wants to speak English with them but
their employer is putting her off. She has been reading more
from Vetëvendosje! and she's starting to agree with what they
say, although she's yet to make this public, especially to her
family.

The American girls have learnt Albanian for their job and
they're trying it out tonight. They all laugh as they mispro-
nounce the words and she is drawn in to the laughter, the
excitement of the evening, drawn in to making the most of
the night before she has to go back to her town tomorrow and
help her father with his market stall.

The British guy is tall and thin and his ears stick out a little. She supposes that this might be common in Britain and she thinks that at least he has a friendly smile, to make up for his ears. He seems a rather serious sort of guy, older than the twenty-two he says he is, and he starts asking her all about the war and she gets annoyed because she doesn't know everything there is to know about the war and also because she's more than that. She's more than just some war stories. And she tells him. And he looks sorry and impressed all at the same time. And he asks her if she can forgive him for being so terribly rude. 'I'm just so in love with your country,' he says. 'I've been here nine months now and it's like an addiction. For me, this is the best place in the world.'

She enjoys his enthusiasm. She likes that he is actually interested. They argue about Vetëvendosje! He says he gets it, but he isn't sure what they actually do believe in, apart from tearing down what the UN is trying to do. 'And really, nationalism, is that the answer?' he says.

She likes the fact that he isn't afraid to challenge them. She likes his smile. She even likes his interest in the war.

On their way home, the other girls tease her about him, asking her if she likes guys with British accents and sticking-out ears.

She cannot sleep all night. She takes out her pen and paper and begins to write.

Prayer Time

THE MUSLIM WASHES his hands. Scrubs. Makes sure there is no unclean thing there. And his face too. His lips and the top of his angled cheeks. And his feet in a bowl of water, not hot enough for his liking, but clean and fresh and good to do the job.

He washes his mind too. Scrubs out the anger he felt this morning when the farmer from the next village did not buy his sheep. And the sideways look he gave the farm girl. And he lathers up to rid himself of the terrible laziness he had when he did not go to pick up the child, even when his wife was sore and tired.

He did not sweep the floor before he did all this and now he must sweep and wash again and then stand and raise his hands. Allah in his head and in his mouth. *Allahu Akbar. You are most great. You are most great. You are greatness*, his mouth whispers with familiarity yet so much meaning.

The Christian walks to the table. He pulls the drawer open and his hands search inside for the matches. A cloth, paper, pens – there, the matches. There they are. He lights the candle and stares at it for a second or two, breathing in the delicious smell of smoke, a little luxury of sensation in a busy day.

He prepares himself. Breathes. Tries to focus on God. He thinks of a shepherd. The wise, gentle shepherd carefully leading him through the valley of death. He tries to forget the argument he had with the delivery boy just yesterday, about the manner in which the parcel should arrive. He turns his face to the side, ashamed, thinking of the fact that he did not make the journey to the village where his mother lives last weekend, just because he did not want to. He remembers how he, instead, spent the day reading his book about theology.

He kneels, just so his attitude is right. *Our father in heaven,* he begins, *hallowed be thy name. Your name is hallowed, you are holy, you are greatness,* his lips say with solemnity but lightness too.

The Muslim's hands are folded now, over his chest, and he is distracted for the moment by the regular beating of his heart, the sustainer of his life and that which he does not notice except in quiet times like these. He begins to recite the first chapter of the Quran, in rhythm with his beating heart, and with the same pace and feeling in the words that he has used every day since he was six years old. He remembers how his father taught him this first chapter. How, when they walked to the fields each morning and each evening, he would learn a little bit more. He remembers how the words became a comfort and a ritual and how his mind and lips could separate and come together many times in these regular recitations.

The Christian, still kneeling, lays his hands on the bed and lifts his palms towards God. Strange, now, how those same tiny hands that quavered when holding the huge family Bible have grown so large and heavy. He looks at his hands and follows the veiled blue veins that run from the edges of his body to the centre. Like God's love, he thinks, in every part of me, flowing in and flowing out. *Your kingdom come, your will be done, on earth, as it is in heaven,* he says. *Your will be done, your will be done,* he repeats over and over and over and over, creating a regular rhythm, the words swelling with more meaning each time they are uttered.

The Muslim raises hands again, then bows and follows all that is necessary. *Allah is great. Glory be to Allah. Allah hears those who call upon him. Allah be praise to you.* He praises Allah daily, at the right time, not like those who have turned away, because he knows that Allah is love. Allah loves him and gives him grass and breath and life and food. He is not destitute, on the streets, like some others. He is grateful to Allah and will thank him all the days of his life. He will praise his God who, like his heart, sustains his life and keeps his legs walking, his arms carrying, his hands mending and his animals providing. *Allah is great, he is greatness, he is to be praised.*

The Christian follows the rhythms of the prayer he learned when he was just a child. *Give us this day our daily bread and forgive us our sins, as we forgive those who sin against us. And lead us not into temptation and deliver us from evil.* He knows he has had more than his share of daily bread and of this he is acutely aware and intensely grateful. *Forgive my sins,* he begs God. He knows his sins would not seem many to some, but he knows that he has not been pushed to hurt or steal or lust or betrayal. He thanks God for the safety from distraction, the keeping from pain, the distance from illness he has felt. *God is great, he is greatness, he is to be praised.*

They both, now calm and focused, kneel and think of others.

The Muslim thinks of Fahri, the neighbour of his brother, too sick to tend the land and grey and almost fading. And of Fahri's wife who smiles but really is just holding on, her face like water. And he asks for Allah's peace.

The Christian thinks of Boro, the man with just one leg,

who comes to sit at church each Sunday and cries during the hymns. And of Boro's mother who chose to bring him up alone rather than to give him up. And he asks for God's peace.

The Muslim has an ache in his heart for his wife, who would like another child, before she is too old, but who every month is disappointed. And he asks for Allah's peace.

The Christian thinks of his mother, alone now, save for him and the neighbour Stefan, and of her stiff hands and the heart she tries to keep from bitterness. And he asks for God's peace.

And both these men, breathing in the air they are a little more grateful for, step out into the world with a little more love to give and a little more patience with themselves and others and with a little more hope that things will not turn from bad to worse as people say they will. They both sigh and hope that they won't have to make the kinds of choices no man wants to make. They both pray a silent, final prayer that God will help them to do what will need to be done and what will cause less evil and less pain and less suffering in this world.

How to Bring up a Kosovan Girl

H ER LITTLE GIRL is beginning to play. She make-be-
lieves houses and mothers and fathers and making cake.
She likes to dance to Albanian music, bending her knees and
clapping her hands. The Kosovan husband brings her hair
bands and dolls and little sweet treats. She can see that he
loves his daughter and that she melts his heart in a way that
the Kosovan Wife has never been able to. Well, not unless you
count the brief months of honey at the beginning.

He scoops her up when he is not working and cradles her
in his arms. '*Bukur*, sweet, gorgeous,' he says to her. 'You are
the most beautiful girl in the world,' he says. 'Daddy's little
sweetheart,' he croons. 'I will always protect you,' he insists.

She likes this in a way. She cannot deny that she likes it.
She likes to see him loving her and she likes to see that this
man has this in him. *It is not all money and pride and guns,*
she thinks. *There is love and glow and enjoyment.* She is glad.
She does not know how to make this seep into their relation-
ship, but she is glad.

Her little boy is getting bolder. He speaks in sentences and
asks her about everything. 'Why do the chickens peck my legs?
Why are we going to grandmother's? Where is Daddy? When
can we have another story?'

She decides that he must learn to write. She writes out
letters for him to copy and soon he can write his name. He
enjoys the movement of the pencil, the curves of the rounded

letters, moving his hand up and down for the taller letters: *just like me*, she thinks, *he is just like me.*

One evening they visit her parents-in-law and there is a plastic truck that the little boy is playing with. The little girl likes this too and soon there is an argument, tears, a telling-off. The Kosovan husband gives her something else to play with.

Later in the evening, they watch a cousin's wedding video. 'Look at the dresses,' her mother-in-law says to the Kosovan Wife's daughter. 'Aren't they pretty?' Both children stand in front of the TV and begin to dance to the music. They turn and twist and giggle. It brightens them all.

'One day this will be you,' they say to the little girl. 'You will have a beautiful dress and a big party.' The Kosovan Wife wants to speak, cannot speak, wants to speak.

When the children are asleep, she creeps into the room. She looks at her little girl. She watches her breathing, her face full of life, her little fingers full of potential. She prays, silently, that the next one will be a boy.

The Maiden in the Box

THE BOY ARRIVED at his Godfather's and was grateful to realise that his Godfather was a kindly man, with a business and an elegant house. He had no wife and no children and so enjoyed the boy's company, treating him as if he was his own son.

He made him a comfortable bed with a thick blanket and he told the boy that he must cook for him each day. 'This is your job,' the Godfather said. 'I have no wife or daughters to cook for me, so you must do this. You will also look after my shop each day and see that everything is in place.'

The boy took his job very seriously. Each day he walked to the market and bought peppers and tomatoes and cabbage and spices. Each night he tried to cook the meals that his mother had cooked but he had never been taught how, so, although they were edible, they were never exactly as he had wanted to make them. But the boy grew stronger with all this food and with exercise and with employment. And he grew happier too, for with his wages he was able to send money to his mother and he was able to save a little too.

How to Attract an English Boyfriend

THANKFULLY HE'S THERE again the next week. She's tried not to think of him all week but she keeps going over what she should have said to him, what she could have said to him, what she will say to him, if she ever sees him again.

And she is given the chance. He's already there in the bar with her friends and he definitely looks at her when she arrives. He definitely gives her more of a glance than he gives anyone else. Or is she just imagining it? Is he just the same to everyone? Is she just making this up to make herself feel better?

She decides to sit away from him. If he likes her, he'll find a way of coming to sit nearer. She knows this. So she says hello and moves away and then he gets up to get a drink and then he is there. Next to her, his shirt touching her arm and his voice saying that he's been looking forward to speaking to her again. *She has such interesting views, she has such a great way of telling him things, she has such a lovely face.*

They speak to each other all evening. The others raise their eyebrows at her and giggle. The others say to her that it is as if no one else is there.

'Don't be silly,' she says. 'It is nothing,' she says. But she knows it isn't nothing. But she knows that this is everything.

And they talk about her stories. And he wants to read them. And she tells him all about the interviews she is doing and about the two stories she is working on right now. And he wants to read them even more. And he wants to read them even more.

They arrange to meet next Wednesday evening. He says he wants to meet her to read her stories, just the two of them. 'Do you have a boyfriend?' he asks. *Of course not,* she thinks, *I am the Returned Girl.* And she just says, 'No. No, I don't.'

And on the way home, she worries about her father. She thinks about the kindness he has shown her. She knows that not every father would have done what he has done. And she swishes his pride at her marks around in her head. She remembers his pride and his delight and his kind, old eyes, wrinkled at the edges.

She imagines his eyes changing: disapproving, disappointed, disbelieving. And she feels a little guilty. But she is still going to go. The Returned Girl knows that she must do this.

Hospitals Before the War

YOU HAVE A sick father. He has cancer of the bowel and it hurts him to eat, to move, to laugh, to breathe. You watch him rasping and yelping in his sleep. You watch him trying to smile with the grandchildren and thanking his wife for her care. You know that it will not be long. And you know that it cannot be helped. Cancer just will get you sometimes; it cannot be stopped; it is not the enemy's fault. Even though you think that those strangers want you all to suffer, they did not inflict this particular suffering.

But the doctors will not help you. You ask for help; they do not come. But the hospitals will not help you. You ask for drugs; they will not provide. Everyone who speaks your language and who loves your imploring eyes has been turned away from the hospital and you are left asking, with no one to listen.

It's not that you have money. You don't. But you gather every coin, every note, empty every bank account, ask every relative living abroad to send you some, because you do not want to see him suffer. If you cannot get a doctor, you will get drugs from somewhere. 'Let there be less pain, let there be less pain,' you pray over his body.

You give everything you have for medicines and bring them home. And there are organisations who have helped. And they give you drugs for your father too.

And you are able to help him to glide from this world to

the next, not to judder, not to writhe in pain, not to shiver and to shake and to scream. You gave him that much. You did all that you could.

Factories Before the War

H E COULD NOT read and write but he could fix. He could twist the wires in a machine to make them work again and knew which place to oil and which part to remove. He knew how to listen for a grinding engine or a misplaced cog or a faulty lever.

At school he hadn't done well. They liked him well enough but the letters on the page danced and moved and words wouldn't stay in his head. He'd always been good at drawing cars and he'd drawn them over and over and could make the sound of seven different types of engine.

So, when he was fourteen, because he had two older brothers who would work on the land, he started to work at the factory. And he was pleased with this. And he was satisfied.

Just sweeping at first. Around the machines and the men and the movement and the motors. He swept happily, listening to the sounds of the clicking and the buzzing. Singing along to the humming and the clunking. Moving to the rhythm of the engines and dancing in between the workers in a sort of mechanical waltz.

And then he was allowed to grease the machines, to tend to their cares, to nurture them and heal their ills. Sometimes he just had to listen and to give a nudge. Sometimes just a pea-sized blob of oil could get a giant machine going again. Sometimes it took hours of careful disassembling then reassembling again. It was a labour of love. It was a labour of love.

They joked about how he wasn't married. Said that he was too in love with the engines to ever share his heart with a woman. At night he dreamt of racing cars, of tractor wheels, of vast imagined machines – he awoke to the gentle buzz of an engine in his ears.

And when the troubles really began to start and they sent him home and told them all that there were to be no Albanians in this factory now, that they no longer had any jobs, his sorrow wasn't just the sorrow of losing your money, of being rejected from an employment, of losing purpose, of feeling betrayed. It was heartbreak. Like when a lover breaks your heart into pieces and you can never put them back together in the same way again. Like when your wife leaves you for another man and you will never feel her soft body next to yours in bed, will never see her eyes in the morning, will never hear her greeting you again as you walk into your kitchen each evening.

At night, he ached for the feel of the metal. His clean arms longed to be greasy and dirty and useful. His ears longed for the sound of engines singing.

How to Want a Kosovan Baby

STRANGE, ISN'T IT, how when you decide you want
something, you don't always get it? How what you didn't
want comes so easily, but how what you want doesn't always
occur.

She doesn't know why this baby is resisting being created.
Nothing is different, she tells herself. *Nothing is different.*

But she knows that she didn't want the last one and maybe
that is why this one just won't come. But she must have this
baby to take the other's place. But she must have this baby to
take the other's place.

She prays to God each night. 'Give me another baby,' she
says. 'Give me another baby,' she begs. 'Give me another baby,'
she pleads. She was told, when she was a little girl, that God
could do anything, but she doesn't see this happening. She
wonders if he listens, if he cares, if he wants to do anything
to make it better. She tells God that she wants another baby,
needs another baby. *I must create another in place of the other,*
she thinks, *that would be right. It would be what God wanted.*

By day she looks after the other two. She feeds them, plays
with them, walks them round the edges of the land, always
stopping to remember the baby who died.

'Where did the baby go?' her little boy asks.

'Just to heaven,' she says. 'Just to heaven.'

'Why did the other baby die?' her little boy asks her.

'Only God knows,' she says. 'Only God knows.'

But inside she knows. *I didn't want him enough*, she thinks, keeps on thinking, over and over. *I didn't hold on to him enough*, she thinks, keeps on thinking, over and over.

She makes food for the family and her mother-in-law visits most days. She helps her to beat out the carpets and to cook her bread and she plays with her grandchildren. She listens to the Kosovan Wife as she tells her children their stories.

'You're good at that,' the mother-in-law says. 'The children love your stories.'

The Maiden in the Box

ONE HOT DAY, the boy was sitting outside the shop in the shade, watching as the townspeople went by. He saw beggars and rich men, mothers with lines of children trailing behind like ducklings, soldiers and shopkeepers and wandering tradesmen. It was a quiet day for him and there had been only two customers in the shop.

A tradesman walked past, carrying a huge wooden box and shouting out, 'Box for sale! Box for sale! If you buy this box you might regret it, but if you don't buy it, you'll regret it too!' The boy was so curious. What was in the box? Why was it being sold? Why was the tradesman being so mysterious?

He asked the tradesman how much the box would cost to buy. 'The box will cost you two hundred lek,' said the tradesman. 'It is a good price and what is inside is much more valuable than the money you will pay for it.'

The boy had managed to save just two hundred lek. *It must be a sign that I should buy the box*, he thought to himself. He was excited to have money he had saved and he was excited to have money to spend. Never before had the boy ever bought anything just for himself.

'Okay, I'll take it,' he said to the tradesman.

He carried the box inside the house and placed it in a dark and dusty corner so that his Godfather didn't see it. He didn't want his Godfather, who had been so kind to him, to think that he had wasted his wages on a box. But buying that box had been something that he hadn't been able to resist.

How to Have an English Boyfriend

IT IS WEDNESDAY. She tells her aunt that she is going out with some friends and she spends time brushing her long, dark hair. She looks in the mirror and is sure that she looked better yesterday, the day before, but not today. She is sure her nose is not quite straight and her chin sticks out too much. She did not notice these things yesterday, but today they seem quite obvious.

She decides not to go. She can leave him waiting in the coffee shop and he will think that something important has come up. That's right, she will not go. There are plenty of other girls he can meet up with. He will find someone else. Someone with a better nose. Someone with a normal chin.

But then, she remembers being returned. She remembers that she is not the girl who just does nothing and accepts the name she is given. She remembers the nights of study and the stories. She remembers.

She gathers the printed stories in a folder and puts them in her bag. She can always say she has forgotten them. She can always pretend.

She gets there early. *Better to be waiting for him*, she thinks, *reading* The Hunger Games *and sipping on a drink. Yes, better for him to see me and I can pretend I have not been waiting long, am engrossed in my book, did not see him walking towards me, although I will see him, I will detect his every move, of course.*

She orders a macchiato and sips it, whilst staring at her book and remembering the other possibility. Perhaps he will not come. Perhaps he will leave her there and has changed his mind. Perhaps he has already met someone with a straighter nose, a less pointy chin, and he is with her tonight. Of course, that is what will happen. She will wait just a little bit longer and then go home. Of course, he will not come. Why would he?

And there he is, walking along the main street, looking a little crumpled but smiling and he has come, he has turned up. She is not the Disappointed Girl. She breathes in and pretends not to notice him. She begins to read ferociously.

He says hello and nice to see her again and can he buy her a drink. And she says yes to another coffee and she still keeps breathing while he orders a coffee from the waiter.

And then there are five minutes of polite conversation. And then they remember each other and begin to talk and talk. And he asks to read her stories. And she is not sure. But she gives them to him anyway and he says he will return them, when he has read what she has written. He takes the folder so carefully, so gently, as if it is a little bird with a broken wing. He promises to read them and to tell her what he thinks.

A Decomposing Body in a House

THE SOLDIERS HAD shot him dead and he lay there in the house alone. No one to prepare him for his final journey to the earth. No one to gather him up and cocoon him in a layer of blanket. No one to whisper a final prayer over his body and to bow their heads and place a hand over their heart in a final act of sorrow. Unprotected in life and unprotected in death, he lay, arms splayed out exactly as they were in that final moment when life was taken from his unprepared lips and his arms made their final act of protest. Too soon, too carelessly, too cruelly his life was taken.

And now, cold and alone and greying, he lies there on the floor of the kitchen where only the cockroaches feed and where only the silent house knows about this solitary occupant.

No burial, no ritual, no goodbye. Just a terrified scream and nothing. They even took away his chance for mourners, as if taking his life wasn't enough already.

His family will find him there, in about two months, and the image of his decomposing body will be the final insult that these soldiers will give to his children as their inheritance.

The Grain Tower

IT IS TALL and imposing, like a giant man guarding the skyline of the town. It is grey and solid and square. It is bold and upright and reaches into the air. It holds grain in its silver containers and it is useful.

They do not necessarily like this building, but it is familiar and certain, as is the regular milk from the cows and the words to be careful from your father and the inevitable patterns of coming and going that weave in and out of a lifetime.

And when the difficulties start to get more threatening, the tower seems to loom more menacingly, casting a shadow of darkness over the town. Its shadow represents the real shadow in their minds and they live in fear of greyness and deadening and the uniformity to come.

When the darkness really does spread and the danger is real and is not just a spectre in everyone's minds, the tower becomes part of their horror. The soldiers climb up it and claim it as a grey symbol of their oppression. They load their guns and kill audacious old men scurrying quickly to buy their bread. They shoot down women who dare to hang their sheets in the back garden. They murder a neighbour who hurries next door to give a jar of peppers to her friend in a bold and outrageous act of kindness.

The tower becomes the enemy, their most giant recruit, a tall signal that this town is under occupation. *Look at me*, it says. *I am grey and menacing and frightening. You are never out of sight. I watch out for you and see you everywhere you move.*

Later, when it is all over, the tower remains. They do not knock it down and try to forget those who died at its hands. They leave it as a horrible monument of what has been, the dark reminder at the back of their minds that this terror could come uninvited again.

The Farmers

FORTY-FIVE FARMERS. THEY are hard-working men, with blisters on their hands and well-developed muscles. Most of them can smell the rain before it comes. They can select a patch of ground and know where things will grow and things will not. They are gentle with the cows, leading them to the best places to graze. They can grow tomatoes that taste of the sun. Their yellow peppers, translucent almost, are that most special mix of bitter and sweet. They live outside, they love their land, they produce for their family, their people, their loves.

One farmer may have a son. Just a young son, say four or five, who he looks at with a melted butter heart. One farmer may have three daughters, his pride; they are fiercely beautiful, clever, bold; he would give his life for these girls. Another farmer has a wife who is the deepest source of joy for him; she lives in his heart like the seed that he plants deep within the soil. They all have parents and most have taken over the family farm, that most precious of inheritances; their privilege in life is to tend this special gift.

Of course, they are ordinary men. One quarrels with his wife over the taste of the flija and the broken cupboard in the kitchen. Another has a baby that screams all night and he is tired, so tired, so, so tired. Parents can be interfering; arguments are had; there is sometimes not enough money to stretch to the vulnerable mouths. There is sorrow; there is joy.

They are humans, shaped by desire and longing. Of course.

I do not want you to think that these men are not ordinary. They are. They are dirty, sweaty, working men. They hide their feelings with gruffness, kiss the soft bodies of their wives, love their children with a passion as far as the stars. There is nothing in them that makes them extraordinary.

Forty-five farmers.

Forty-five farmers. Visited.

Told to leave their houses. To go to the centre of town. To dip their heads and lower their eyes and say their prayers because, sneeringly, they are told, this day could be your last. Ha ha. The last, they are told. Ha ha. Ha ha. Laugh, come on, laugh!

They laugh, mechanically. Laughing is the furthest thing from their minds.

One objects. He is kicked in the head but he still is made to stand and gather. To laugh and forcibly smile through horror-filled face and a stomach that is churning with anxiety.

What is it these grey, domineering men want? What are they doing? What poison has overtaken their minds and their hearts and their souls and their bodies to perform this evil?

Only God can know. Only God can know.

They are made to march. Faster. Slower. March. Stop. Gun in your back, a kick in your shin, saliva in your face, a shove into the mud and then an instruction to stand to this one or to that one.

This one vomits by the side of the road. He is slapped.

That one is crying but with silent yelps. His friend wipes his tears so they do not see.

Faster, faster, upwards, upwards. Walk. Keep moving. Don't stop or we'll shoot you.

Keep moving you filthy creatures. Don't look back or I'll blow your brains out.

Look at me that way again and you'll be sorry.

Keep moving. Walk. Move. Don't stop or we'll shoot you.

They shot them anyway. Forty-five farmers. Gentle men. Taken to the top of the hill and shot down dead.

That'll teach you for loving the earth, for enjoying the pleasure of your wife's angled face when she kissed you, for daring to be gentle to the sheep and the cows and the children and the soil.

That will teach you for rearing chickens and producing enough for your family to eat, with a little left over for your neighbours and a few things to sell in the market at the end of the day.

You have ended your days with a bullet in your head. You lie there on the top of the mountain with the snow and the wind and the grass your only witnesses.

Perendi ke meshire per ne. God have mercy. God have mercy.

God have mercy, the wind whistles to no one.

How to Have a Kosovan Argument

H E H A S B E E N to the mosque to pray that morning and he has taken their little boy too. Her little girl sleeps for two hours and she has this time to herself. *For once, for once.*

The Kosovan Wife makes herself a thick, sweet Turkish coffee, she sits at the table and lays out her notebook, where she has begun to write out the stories she tells her children each night. She does not want to forget them, wants to pass them on, wants to give them to her children as a gift.

We must pass on our stories, she thinks.

Just like her little boy, she enjoys the marks that she makes when she presses hard on the page and writes deliberately, slowly, or in the scrawling hand she uses when her mind races faster than her arm. She draws little pictures of what is happening in the tale and she forgets everything else.

Only the maiden and the box and the boy and the Godfather exist. She draws the boy's tiny little eyes, his scruffy clothes, the sad embrace when he says goodbye to his mother.

'What are you doing?' the Kosovan husband says, when he returns. She hasn't heard him, meant to put this all away, is annoyed with herself for getting lost in the work.

'I'm just writing the stories for the children,' she replies, thinks he won't mind, is scared that he might.

He looks at them. He says that they are good. He stays silent for a while.

'Is this why you are taking the pill?' he says.

'Is this why you are trying to stop us from having another child?' he says.

She tells him she is not, has not, wants a child, is disappointed it hasn't happened yet.

'But,' he says, 'the others happened so quickly. There is no reason why this one hasn't formed.'

He looks at her writing again.

'I prayed this morning to God,' he says, 'and asked him, why doesn't my wife have another child? And I return and find you doing this. Is this my answer? Are you stopping yourself because you want to spend your time doing this?'

'No, no,' she answers, 'No, of course, not. No.'

'My mother keeps asking me,' he says, 'why we don't have another one, and I say that I don't know. I don't know. Well, maybe now I know.'

He is angry. The little boy is crying. The little girl wakes up, crying too.

He shouts at her and says that she must focus on the family. He takes the notebook away and puts it in a box on top of the wardrobe. 'You must think of the children,' he says. 'Think of another baby,' he says.

'But it is for the children,' she says. 'It is for the children.'

The Maiden in the Box

THE NEXT DAY was a Friday and the boy went early to the market to buy all the ingredients for the dinner. He bought peaches and apples, lamb and tomatoes, a big bag of rice and some bitter spices. *I will make a delicious meal*, he thought, *to say thank you to my Godfather for all that he has done.*

The boy went back to his Godfather's house and placed the bag of ingredients on the kitchen table, ready to be prepared. The boy went firstly to the mosque to say prayers and then he intended to returned to the house to cook.

When he opened the door of his Godfather's house again, he could smell something so appetising. He followed this most wonderful smell and found a stew sitting in the pan, cooked to perfection. It was brown and thick and bubbling and smelt of sitting inside by the fire on a cold winter's day. He thought that his Godfather must have seen the ingredients and must have made it and he felt a little unhappy that he had not been able to say thank you to his Godfather in this way. But the food was steaming and smelled pungent and spicy and ready to eat. The boy served the stew up for them and placed it in big, round metal dishes.

The meal tasted incredible. The lamb was so tender that it melted in the boy's mouth, the tomato sauce was thick and spicy and sweet all at the same time. His Godfather said, 'This meal is fit for a king. All your practice has paid off; you will soon get a job as a head chef in a hotel, I think.'

The boy thought that his Godfather must have been making fun of him. After all, the Godfather must have made this appetising food himself and the boy was embarrassed that he had never been able to cook anything as good as this for his Godfather. He said nothing and felt ashamed and regretful that he was not a good cook at all. He was truly sorry that he had not been able to thank his Godfather by cooking this wonderful dish himself.

How to Take a Kosovan Picture

S HE SEES HIM a few times a week. She enjoys having someone to meet, someone who is interested in just her. And he eats up her stories like he is a child and they are sweets. 'You must write, when you've finished university,' he says. 'You must write.'

He tries to catch her hand as they walk around the city but she always moves it away, always shrugs off any public affection. *Not yet, not yet.*

They walk along Bill Clinton Boulevard and stare up at the statue. 'I used to think he was the greatest man who ever lived,' she says. She notices the confident way the statue stands, as if his raised arm was just waving goodbye to all the Serbian troops and as if his wave was enough, as if it hadn't involved bombings and gunshots and pain.

'Yeah, he and Tony Blair aren't quite so popular outside of Kosovo,' he says. They also see the utilitarian-style Vetëvendosje! graffiti behind the bronze Clinton in capital letters, JO NEGOCIATA VETËVENDOSJE! 'That's what *your* party thinks,' he teases.

She doesn't like the way he talks about Vetëvendosje! like they are a joke or something. 'They're a good party,' she says, 'they mean something to us.'

'I know, I know, I'm just joking around with you,' he says, but she knows that he's part of what Vetëvendosje! is working against, working for UNMIK, and she's not sure that he actually takes them seriously.

They walk behind the newborn statue and he takes her picture there again. How many times has she had her picture taken there? Yet she always enjoys it, always wants another. *Newborn addiction*, she thinks. *Addiction to being newborn*, she thinks. She isn't like the other girls she knows; she won't post it on Facebook. She just wants these pictures up in her bedroom. They make her feel stronger, more alive, renamed.

They walk into the bright shopping centre behind the statue and sit down in the central coffee shop which is so modern and trendy and European, she thinks. It has curved chairs and sofas covered in alarmingly bright fabrics, and it serves all sorts of drinks you can't get in her town. They both order bambis and sit too close to each other in a lime-green scooped chair. His long, gangly legs don't fit under the table well and he keeps shifting about.

A friend from her class at university comes by and they kiss each other's cheeks and she introduces the English boyfriend as her English friend. 'A very handsome friend to spend time with,' the girl says in Albanian, laughing and going on her way. 'Does your family know?' This is the things she hates about her country. *Everyone knows you, everyone has an opinion, everyone makes comments, everyone talks about you.*

She slurps her bambi up quickly and says she needs to go. 'Will I see you tomorrow evening?' he says. 'There's a film at the cinema I want to take you to, about a Kosovan soldier after the war. I think you'll like it.' She agrees to meet him.

That night, under the covers in her aunt's apartment, she itches and scratches and dreams of her life in England with him. They have a house and a new car and a child and she has books and books and books to read. The books keep piling up around the house and they become the furniture, the floors. They eat off book plates and then the book piles become higher and higher, until they're coming out the windows and they can no longer actually open the front door to get in. She wakes and writes uneasily, in the middle of the night.

The Girlfriend

I TRIED TO come to you. I tried to see you before we had to go. I tried to untangle myself from my family and the planning and the worries and the packing. But I could not; it was too dangerous; I might have been seen and the soldiers are merciless these days.

Sometimes it feels like death would be better than leaving you, but that is foolishness and just the terrible thinking that this situation has driven me to. But I cannot bear to leave you. I cannot bear to leave you, darling.

We are all fleeing, just like every other family in this town. There are so many rumours about what will happen to us if we stay. They drip like poison into my mind.

It isn't safe and, even though I don't want to leave you like this, I have to go. I do not blame you at all for this. Please know that I love you with my whole heart and know that I do not blame you at all. I know you wish us peace. I know you wish us love.

I want to go back to how things were. Before this nightmare descended. Before our love was impossible and before people told us who we could and couldn't share a coffee or a joke or a feeling with. There is so much rage in people's hearts, so much anxiety, there is violence I didn't know existed – how can anything ever be the same?

I will pray for the day when I can once again see your face. I will refuse to say goodbye to you and I will refuse to let them decide that we cannot have a future. I hope that one day we can make plans again, the plans that are so precious to our hearts. Be safe, my love.

The Boyfriend

L ATE LAST NIGHT I watched in horror as a procession of vehicles drove into the hills. And I knew that you must be there, somewhere, *zemer*. Foolish of me, but I pretended that one of the lights fading into the distance was you. It's romantic, silly, childish even. I pray to my God for you for each minute, each hour, each day. My people, sending out your people as if they were wild animals. We are enemies, you and I. But I say to myself, how can I love my enemy so dearly?

I know that you will never read this letter, but I wanted to write to you, to feel that your heart is beating somewhere, somewhere in those mountains.

Darling, I am strangely grateful that you are gone. If you saw what has happened in our town you would never stop crying. The school has been burnt down, the hospital is full of soldiers and they act as if they have no eyes to see the pain they cause, no hearts to feel what others endure; they are drunk every night and it is as if they revel in the suffering. People scamper around; everyone is afraid of everyone else. Everything has turned to grey: the food, people's faces - even the air has a sort of greyness to it.

And I am lucky because I am not the enemy. But even I cannot trust anyone. I saw a dead body on the road yesterday and I wanted to lie down in the street beside it and die myself.

I cannot believe that it has come to this. I cannot believe that your people are expelled and hurt in my name. Be safe, my love.

How to Go on a Kosovan Holiday

THERE IS A new road, straight to Albania, and everyone is going there for the holidays. The Kosovan Wife's in-laws have relatives who live in Sarandë and they will stay with them and they will be away for two weeks. 'Just the right time for us all to go on a holiday,' they say. 'Just what we all need. Time to relax, time to get some sun, time to be together as a family.'

She has never seen the sea before. She's been to the lake and to swimming pools to swim but she's never seen the coast. Only in pictures on the internet. The thought of the holiday actually excites her and she is glad to give her children the chance to feel the sand beneath their toes. She is glad to give herself the chance to feel the sand beneath her toes.

The apartment is just two streets from the beach and they go there every day. She lies on the warm sand and lets the hot grains warm up her skin. She feels like a piece of bread toasting comfortably under the grill. Her mother-in-law looks after the children while she sleeps and she feels the best she has felt in a while.

Swimming in the sea is a new pleasure. She loves to walk out to sea and swim as far as she can, with her back to the beach, with her back to the land, with her back to her family. As she floats and feels the water all around her, she forgets everything and just feels surrounded. The sun on her face makes her squint her eyes and she melts into the landscape. *If*

I die, she thinks, *I want to be thrown out to sea. This is where I belong.*

She's been out swimming for at least half an hour and she guesses she should go back. She can see her family in miniature on the beach and she sees her husband playing with the children, running around and chasing them. *He is good like that*, she reminds herself, *he is good in so many ways. I must remember this*, she thinks, *I must not be difficult, ungrateful.*

As she moves back towards the beach she sees her little boy being swung by her husband. He loves that, enjoys the thrill of flying through the air. She smiles, hears his giggles in the distance, reminds herself again that her husband is not so bad.

Then, she sees him pick him up and throw him in the water. 'That's dangerous,' she calls, but she's too far away. She starts swimming frantically. She doesn't want him to do that. She needs to get there, quickly, faster, quickly. 'He can't swim,' she's calling, 'don't do that!' But she's too far away.

She hears the boy giggle but now the husband is picking him up again and this time he throws him further. 'No, no, stop it, no.' She's thrashing about and her chest is getting tighter. She's trying to get there, but the sea is holding her back. She's moving her arms but getting nowhere and her chest is getting tighter.

The Maiden in the Box

T HE BOY WAS determined to thank his Godfather with
a delicious meal. Early the next morning he went to the
docks and bought a slippery fish from the market. It had a
silvery body that flashed like a rainbow in the sunlight. He
wrapped it in paper and laid it in the cool of the kitchen whilst
he went out and did some deliveries for his Godfather's shop.
He intended to cook it for their lunch.

When the boy returned there were neighbours outside the
house, smiling and joking with him. 'I'm going to get you to
marry my daughter,' said one woman, 'if you can cook like
that, we definitely want you in our family!'

The boy could smell the delicious aroma of griddled fish
and vegetables coming from his Godfather's house. He and
his Godfather sat down to the best lunch they had ever tasted.
The Godfather kept telling the boy how wonderful his cooking
was and so the boy knew that his Godfather was not making
fun of him and had not cooked it himself. The boy was so
puzzled: who was cooking these delicious meals for them?

How to Take Part in Kosovan Activity

S HE REMINDS HERSELF, over and over, that it is her
life and that she must do what feels right to her. She walks
to the meeting place and her chest is tight, nervous, fluttering.
She had said that she would meet them here and that they
would all go together.

There are groups of people walking down the street, mainly
men. Men in leather jackets, men in T-shirts and many of
them smoking cigarettes. Lots of young people too: walking,
discussing, purposeful.

She meets them and they greet each other, but there is a
sense of purpose that doesn't need chat. They look at each
other and they don't need to say a thing. The unspoken rules
are that they will try to stay together and that they will avoid
television cameras. Normally, they would love to be on TV,
but today, they must not, cannot, will try to avoid it.

As they walk towards the parliament building she sees the
shining windows and its height. *It is meant to dazzle, glitter,
intimidate*, she thinks. *Not today, not today.* She also looks
at the statue of Skenderbeg, riding his horse boldly. *We are
Skenderbeg*, she thinks. *We are ready, poised, determined to do
battle.* She looks at his stance. *This is us, this is us.*

There's someone there, telling them where the best place to
stand will be. She sees the silver barricades, solid-flimsy, stopping them from getting close, and she and her friends stand,
wait, listen. It is quiet at first, but then the US ambassador

arrives and there is jeering, shouting, movement. She shouts too, excited to be part of this voice, their voice. She can hear herself shouting and she feels powerful, unafraid. Although her voice is small it is mixed up in this huge, loud, thronging mass of voices. *Like a choir*, she thinks. *A noisy, loud choir of protest.*

And then there is more movement and she is pushed back. There's anger, violence, shouting, taunting. The police start to move forward. There are police with eggs and flour all over them. And then people running, throwing stones, pushing, shoving. The police spray gas and hold up their plastic shields.

Everywhere, everywhere there is anger and she is pushed to the back and her arm is hurt. 'This is no place for a woman, go back,' an older man says to her.

She has no choice now. She is part of a large crowd and she is trapped in the middle. She can see a friend and she calls to him and they pull together, exhilarated but petrified of what is happening. She sees a television camera and quickly turns away. She sees police arresting men just a few metres away and she turns away. She sees a friend from university on the floor with a policeman holding him down. She cannot turn away.

She tries to get near to him, to say something, but it isn't possible. She's swept along by a mass of people shoving and heckling and screaming. Like a small pebble in a river, she is dragged by the current and has no power to choose where she will end up. Eventually the movement stops and she finds herself at the edge of the square.

She moves back, moves away, is afraid, is amazed, is inspired, is exhausted.

That night, at a friend's apartment, they watch news report after news report. They breathe in, knowing they were part of something, feeling their pulses racing again. They breathe out, relieved that their faces are not being flashed across the city, the country, the world.

The Journey into the Hills

'FILL YOUR POCKETS with bread, Ardian. And put on at least three layers of clothes. As many as you can. You must choose your warmest jumpers and thickest socks. Do what I say, as quickly as you can, *zemer,*' said his mother.

He asked her why they must do this, but her face, grey, like the grain silo menacing their town, showed him that there must be no questions.

He obeyed her. Mechanically, he dressed himself, layer after layer, peeling woollen socks up his legs and forcing another T-shirt over the three underneath. He felt warm, suffocated, as fat as the mayor. He wondered how the mayor would fit on so many layers of clothes. There wouldn't be any room, and if the mayor tripped as they walked on the long journey mother had said the whole town was going on, he would roll right back into the town! He would be a ball of clothes and too many baklava, with his face puffing in that red, sweaty way, the way he looked when he made ever so important speeches to the town.

He laughed a little to himself, as he ripped bread from the loaf and began stuffing it into his pockets. How funny, to think of the mayor like that!

'Why are you laughing, Ardian?' said Father. 'This is no time for laughing, no time at all. Be ready. We are leaving.'

Everyone was so angry these days. Their faces so stern, like photographs sent from Albania of distant relatives each year.

Their jaws so fixed and solemn. Their eyes so empty as they barked more orders to him.

Mother, greyer than ever, cross with him all the time, yet each evening, picking him up onto her lap like he was a baby – he wasn't a baby any more, she should know this – and trying to cradle him, with tears in her eyes. Of course, he fought her off. He was a big boy now. He flailed violently against her. She cried and cried and begged him to sit with her for just one night, but he would not be treated like a baby. He scowled at her and told her to leave him alone. He was nearly as tall as Ehad now – she should realise this.

It was all the Serbs' fault, he felt. Everyone was talking about them, and since they'd been introduced into conversation, everyone had gotten sadder and more serious. Since they'd been on everyone's lips, shoulders had hunched and eyes were darting around all the time. He had to stay in, he couldn't see his friends, and even the makeshift school at Uncle's, the one interesting thing in the day, had stopped.

And now this tiresome walk into the mountains with everyone as silent as trees. He just wished things would go back to normal.

The tractor, pulling a trailer full of relatives and neighbours, came by early in the morning. They were waiting by the door and they all, Grandmother included (Grandmother in the back of a tractor!), crammed into the back. They sat on hay bales and bags of clothes; blankets and jars of flour, wheelbarrows, bottles of milk and boxes of turshi were rammed between them. They were like peppers in a jar, squashed and misshapen, he felt, and getting slowly softer and more bruised.

He stood between Grandmother and someone who used to be a policeman, before everything had changed, and tried hard to think of other things. He had a small toy car in his pocket, the paint nearly all scraped from it from years of play, and he felt each ridge on the bottom of the car again and again. He knew father would be cross with him for bringing it. Father said that they must bring bread and that is all, and he knew Ehad would laugh at him, call him a little boy for needing a toy. But for now it was his secret and he flicked the wheels in his pocket, spinning them round and round, trying to forget the jolting beneath him and the policeman's elbow in his shoulder blade.

Grandmother hadn't been well. Since Grandfather had died, an accident at work three weeks ago, her hands had stiffened and she hadn't been cleaning her teeth or washing her face. Ardian had been frightened to go near her recently. The stale breath from her mouth put him off and she seemed to clench him, like a cockerel will clench its perch, if she managed to get hold of him. He had to sleep in the same room as his grandmother and he'd been woken by her screaming Grandfather's name in the night. She shouted curses at some invisible person in her chair in the afternoons. Mother said she was grieving. Ehad and Ardian thought she was going mad.

When they reached the end of the path into the mountains, the path from Bes's uncle's farm, the man driving the tractor told them to get off.

'This is as far as I can take you,' he said.

Family by family, they got down from the trailer. Men pulling wheelbarrows and women pulling small children, they began their slow walk into the hills. They went their separate ways; large crowds could be found, Ardian heard his father say to another man.

Grandmother was finding it difficult. Her legs, unused to

much walking, especially since Grandfather's death, seemed to be seizing up. Father, trying to lead them as fast as he could and telling the children to hurry, slowed to a pace Grandmother could manage.

She tripped over a rock after about half a kilometre. Mother and Father ran to pull her up and Father told Ehad to take Grandmother's arm and lead her.

'I'm holding you back. You must leave me,' she said.

Father told her to stop speaking like a fool and said that all would be well. He said this, but in his eyes Ardian could see a look he had never seen before.

They heard shouting from behind a peak and father told them all to crouch and to be silent. Ardian knew better than to question. He heard the all too familiar language again and heard laughing and gun shots. They stayed very still.

The voices faded and Father, breathing heavily, told them to carry on.

Grandmother, having been crouched against a very cold rock, could not stand again.

'Then you will just have to get into my wheelbarrow,' Father said. He began to move towards her, ready to pick her up.

'And what about the little food you have? And the blankets for the night time?' Grandmother said, 'You'll never survive if you leave them and take me - there isn't room for both.'

'I'll stay here and you come back for me tomorrow, or the next day, on your way down,' she said. 'Leave me blankets and some food and I'll be fine. I will not come with you now. My legs have made their decision.'

Mother told them to keep on walking up the hill, with Ardian leading the way. They were to only go for fifteen metres and then to wait for their parents. They must not look round, as Grandmother must change her clothes, and it wouldn't be right for them to see their grandmother in this way. Mother said this all very cheerfully – the most cheerful thing she'd said in days.

Mother and Father caught them up in a few moments. Mother's eyes, red and sore, stared at the ground, fixedly.

'Mother, why—?'

Father cut him off and said that Mother was not feeling well. He told him to ask no more questions and to keep walking. From his tone, Ardian knew that he must do as he said. Ehad pinched him in the arm and Ardian made a mental note to pinch him back, when it was dark and he would find it harder to return the pain. They kept on walking.

How to Be Rescued

'**Y**OU WERE SO close to shore and then you disappeared,' she can hear him saying to her. 'Why did you go under? What were you doing? Why didn't you just swim back to us? I had to come and get you. It was embarrassing. People were staring at us and you just did it to yourself. There was no reason for it. There was no reason for you to go under the water. What were you thinking?'

He thinks that the more he says, the more he will understand, she thinks. *But he is wrong, but he is wrong.*

She is lying on the beach on a towel. She is breathing. She is taking each breath in and out but she is not speaking. She could speak if she wanted to, but at the moment she chooses to be silent. She is staring at his face. He's fatter than he was, although he still looks young. He has a round face, dark eyes and a stubbly beard which makes him look stylish, fashionable, he thinks. She guesses this is true, what they say about him, that he is handsome and modern. She does not care.

She looks at his body, at the muscles he has and his long legs. *I should be grateful,* she thinks. *He is a good-looking man, he is dark and lean. I should be grateful,* she thinks, *for the children he has given me. I have a new house, I am on holiday, he rescued me from the sea. He is a good father. I should be grateful.*

She tells herself these things whilst looking at him. And he is speaking to her and it sounds like a helicopter whirring over her. And she does not like the way he holds her arm, just a little bit too tightly. And she doesn't like the way he looks at her, as if she has done something wrong.

'I always try to do the right thing,' she says.

He says, 'But you don't.'

She can feel the heat. She lifts her body, turns her head and vomits in the sand.

'You see, you don't. You always do this,' he says.

Her mother-in-law comes over, tries to help her, holds her head, calms the children. 'You're just hot, tired, too much sun,' she says. 'You've just had too much sun out there and then you fainted in the water,' she says. She keeps the children away and sits them with an ice-cream. 'You're just exhausted, or maybe you're pregnant again,' she says, trying to mask any expectation in her voice, but it is there.

The Kosovan Wife stays silent. She says nothing. She sips the water. She wishes that she was still surrounded by the sea.

The Maiden in the Box

THE BOY DECIDED that he must find out who was cooking for them. The next day he went to the market very early and bought courgettes and onions and the whitest of potatoes. He bought a whole chicken and bundles of herbs. He placed all these ingredients in his Godfather's house but, instead of going to the shop, he hid in the cupboard so that he could see who had been making these incredible dishes.

From the cupboard he saw a beautiful woman climb out of the box. She had brown hair, as straight as the tall grasses by the river; she had eyes that flashed a dark and dangerous grey; she had cheeks that reminded him of the mountains in the distance; she moved with an elegance he had never before encountered. She put on an apron and began to cook. She was so happy and so joyful that her presence radiated round the house. He jumped out of the cupboard, kneeled before her and asked, 'Are you a woman or an angel?'

She laughed. A sort of bubbling laugh that made him feel better. 'I'm a woman. Don't be scared,' she said. 'I'm the daughter of the King of Egypt, his only child. I came here on holiday with my father in the summer and I saw you in the town one day and you looked so solemn and so serious and like your eyes were full of stories and I just fell in love with you. My father took me back to Egypt and the plan was for me to marry a prince, but I knew that I was in love with you. I was sure that my father would never let me be with you and so I told him I would never marry. He begged me and scolded me, but I refused to do what he said. My father was so furious with me that he put me in a box and told his servant to take me far away and to sell me to someone. I begged the servant to bring me here and to make sure that he sold me to you.'

How to Listen to a Reaction

WHEN SHE SEES the English boyfriend two days later, he is full of opinions. 'Your party,' he says, in a teasing kind of way. 'Did you see what they did? Did you watch it on television? Did you see what they caused?'

'They organised a protest and, of course, it turned into trouble. Typical! And what are their policies anyway?' he says. 'What will they actually do?' he says. 'They have all these ideals, but no practical promises,' he says. 'They have all these young followers, but they're all just words,' he says. 'Pathetic!' he says. 'Troublemakers! Did you see it, sweetheart, when you were walking to lectures? I hope you didn't see the violence? I hope you didn't get hurt? I hope this hasn't upset you?'

'No, no, English boyfriend, I was not hurt.'

He goes back to watching a news clip on a YouTube channel on his phone. He does not notice her looking at him so carefully. He does not see the sadness in her eyes as she listens to his reaction.

When she returns home that weekend, her father is full of opinions. He, himself, does not want negotiations with Serbia, but he trusts the United States of America. 'They did well for us before,' he says, 'they did what was best. Why would they do any different this time?'

'These foolish people,' he says, 'protesting in Pristina! From the party who are ungrateful for what the United States of

America did for us. From the party who try to cause trouble. From the party who do not support the PDK.'

'Pah!' he says. 'Troublemakers! Did you see it, little chick, when you were walking to lectures? I hope you were not scared? I hope you were not hurt? I hope this did not upset you?'

'No, no, Father, I was not hurt.'

He goes back to watching the news reports on their TV screen. He does not notice her staring at him as he is watching it. He does not see her insides twist as she listens to his reaction.

The Tractor

S HE DID NOT know, when she trained in her twenties, that she would defy death in such a bold and rebellious way. Her job, of course, was life affirming. It took a particular person, practical yet brimming with love, to support these frightened women to bring life into the world.

She had worked at the hospital for over ten years. It was a job that made her humble; each day was a reminder of fragility and pain. But a wonderful employment for a life. Intimate, valuable, spectacular.

Doctor Sheholli was particularly fastidious. He had studied in Belgrade and embraced the most modern of ideas for supporting life.

'I will not have ten women from each family in the room during the birth,' he would order.

'This room will be cleaned after every woman. It must be done.'

'No animals inside my hospital.'

'Each nurse must always wash her hands.'

Some called him controlling and over-zealous. They said he did not love people enough. But she knew he valued people more than anyone ever did. She, in a way, was in awe. A man who made things happen properly. A man who valued life over social niceties. If she had not been married before she was twenty, this would have been the man she would have chosen. And there existed a sort of love, a sort of marriage, between them, he giving orders and she obeying them because she worshipped his passion.

Eight years on, when the darkness fell, she loved him even more. Loved him in the way that she loved her people. Loved him in the way that you would love a saviour.

Eight years on and they knew they all had to go. The constant terror was driving her people mad and the fear of knowing that, at any time, they might come, lived with you like a disease that you could not cure.

When she left, with her own husband and two small children, she took some useful things. She was not naive enough to think that God would seal the wombs. He had not sealed the guns, after all. He had not deadened the seeds of hatred against her people, had he?

These caravans of people, lines of them, leaving for safety. These frightened men and women, craving a haven of protection. They must all go up. Not easy to follow and out of sight. If they could not see them, they would not be offended by their existence. If they could not see them, they would assume someone else had done what they were baying for.

People living side by side, simply, with all they could bring in those few panicked hours. It did not matter how unprepared you were, you must come. It didn't matter if you were half way through making your stuffed peppers and cleaning your bed sheets, you must come. It didn't matter if the fire was still burning, you must come. It didn't matter if your belly was brim-full of a baby, you must come.

And this is where the tractor comes in. A simple farm machine, but useful for climbing up rough terrain. A small wooden carriage attached at the back, used to carrying sheep, but now stuffed with people and belongings and fear and rage and desperate prayers.

The woman's husband came to see her on their second day. His eyes full of tears, he explained how they had heard that she knew what to do. 'You have experience, we beg of you, we need your help, we are terrified.'

Of course, it was always side by side, in love, that they had done this before. Alone, living with her husband and close neighbours in the hills, she did not know if she could do it. But we must wear our faces hard and serious in times like these. Of course, she agreed.

But where? She needed space and privacy, not people living on top of each other, like the animals ready for market day. Not surrounded by buckets and fear and disease and blankets and hatred and clothing and the last few jars of flour and milk.

'I need that tractor,' she told her neighbour.

They cleaned it out, swept, lay down blankets and worked with speed whilst the woman began to scream outside on the grass.

'I know what I'm doing. You have nothing, nothing, to fear,' she told her. Just a young girl, maybe twenty-one, her first child and to be birthing in a situation like this. *What terror, what unexpected suffering*, she thought.

Births are always violent. She saw a beauty in this violence every time, but this birth was spectacular and full of rage and malice and joy like she had not seen.

We will not give up, it said. Each moment closer to birth screamed out to the hills and to the nations of the world that there would be humanity in the darkest of times.

She did not lose a single baby in those months in the hills.

She did not lose a single mother in those dangerous days in that unsuitable tractor.

She did not know that she was born for this. She did not know that love could stretch so far.

How to Annoy Your Husband

A S THE DARKNESS of the winter creeps in again, she begins to chop vegetables up into bright chunks of colour and then she fills pans full of this colour and watches it turn to a brown, delicious-smelling mush that will sustain them into the winter. As she stews vegetable after vegetable, she pours the hot mixture into families of jars. They line up at the back of the kitchen cupboards, ready for the coldest days. She fetches the thicker, warmer, itchier blankets and they make sure that the firewood store is covered and dry. *The snow will be here soon. The snow will be here soon.*

She is still not pregnant.

She has taken to writing and drawing in the afternoon, while the children play. She started in secret, talking the notebook down and replacing it as carefully as she could, but now, she has asked him and he has given her permission. She thinks he sees the greyness in her face. She thinks he doesn't want to be married to a corpse.

She photographs a picture she has drawn with some of her story and she posts it on Facebook. Fifty-two 'likes' straight away.

They comment:

Amazing

I love it!

I didn't know you were a writer

Brilliant, my kids would love this!

She has five new friend requests quickly and she accepts. All have seen her work on another friend's page and she begins to wonder: *Could I do this? Could I do this?*

When he is home, later, her husband is fuming, 'When we were engaged we sorted out your Facebook contacts and now you are accepting requests from men you don't even know? I let you do what you want and this is how you repay me? Why do you embarrass me like this?'

'It was just for my work,' she says, 'just my work. And I don't think there were any men. I didn't think to look . . .'

'No more work,' he says. 'No more writing. It just causes trouble.'

She realises her hands are shaking.

'I have to.'

'Don't be so stupid. What do you mean you have to?'

'I just, I have to do it.'

'Not any more.'

He takes her notebook and her pens and they are thrown into the bins outside.

She says nothing. She does not speak.

'I'm not looking for another man,' she says. 'I just want to write my stories and draw the pictures. That's all I want to do.'

'You're a mother,' he says. 'That should be enough. Why are we not enough for you?'

The Maiden in the Box

WHEN THE BOY heard that this woman was the daughter of the King of Egypt, he did not feel that he was worthy of her. He fell to his knees again and told her this, but she pulled him to his feet and kissed him and assured him that he was the only man she would marry. The boy could not believe it. *That a king's daughter would want to marry me*, he thought to himself, *am I not the most fortunate man alive?*

The daughter of the king and the boy were married, quickly and secretly. They had a ceremony whilst the girl held a simple bunch of white flowers and they asked rough fishermen from the port to be their witnesses. After they were married they bought fresh bread from the baker's shop and ate it with salty butter, licking the melting remains from their fingers and laughing to themselves with happiness. They told no one, not even his Godfather.

The boy went to the port and gave the captain of a ship a box and he issued him with careful instructions. 'Take this box to my mother. Make sure you keep it safe for the whole journey. Inside is precious cargo.'

Of course, inside the box was his wife. He placed a letter to his mother also into the box. The letter stated that this was his wife and that his mother should care for her. As he placed the letter into the box, he touched his wife's hand and promised her that all would be well.

The boy's mother was so surprised when someone

knocked on her door and said that a parcel had arrived for her. *Whatever can it be?* she thought to herself. *Perhaps my son has sent me a present of some china or perhaps he has sent unusual spices from his new home!* Of course, when she opened the box, the mother was amazed and delighted to find inside it a girl, a spectacular girl, wearing a simple white dress and looking nervous and hopeful all at the same time. The girl was holding out a letter and she asked her to read it. 'I hope you will be pleased with what you read,' she said.

When the mother read the letter, tears fell down her cheeks. She was so happy to see her son's writing and so grateful that he had found love. And when she looked at the girl she saw goodness and beauty and mystery and purpose all wrapped up in one human being.

Of course, she looked after the girl and got to know her well and she was delighted with her, in the same way that her son had been. 'My son has married the best woman in the world,' she said, 'and he has given her to me to stop my loneliness. Surely I am the most blessed of women, and when I next set eyes upon my son, nothing will spoil the joy that is rising up within me.'

How to Lose an English Boyfriend

'IT'S NOT BECAUSE of that,' she says.

'It is. You're afraid of what your father will say, what people will think.'

'No. That isn't it.'

'You're afraid that they won't accept me. I know, I've heard about it from other guys in the office with Kosovan girlfriends. No one ever wants to tell their families.'

'That isn't it. You don't know me and you don't know my family.'

'Then, why?'

'Because we are different and I can't see a future.'

She sees she has hurt him. She sees the pursed lips and hears the desperate strain in his voice.

'But, I like you. I don't want to lose you.'

'I think you like my stories,' she says, perhaps a bit too quickly. 'You don't know me as well as you think you do and if you did, you would see that we think differently about Kosovo.'

He doesn't try to argue now. He sits cradling his coffee as if it is his hurt heart. *He's like a child*, she thinks.

She knows that what she says is true because she has thought about it repetitively for nights. Does she want to do this because of her father? Or because she is afraid? But she knows that she is not an afraid person. She knows that if she had to, she could tell them. But she knows that he is not the one she will do this for.

'I'm sorry,' she says.

The Milk

WE FOUND HER, just four months ago, the woman who saved our baby. Her face, so wrinkled with lines. Her eyes hidden, as the skin of her eyelids, now so well worn, sagged over her eyes. I recognised her though. How can one forget such a beautiful face and such a beautiful, shining soul? Her eyes said that she recognised me too, although she hasn't many words these days. Her daughter told me that her voice left her the day that liberation came, as if all her words of ecstasy and joy had floated into the sky in a final celebratory poem and silence was all that was needed ever after. As if there was no more she could utter into this dark, joyous, brutal, unfathomable world. She had seen it all, heard it all and now she had spoken it all too. It made me wonder if we only have so many words allotted to each lifetime - the shy, thoughtful types never using their full quota and the talkative types silenced before their time.

Anyway, we found her. I thought that she would still be in that house, but the fear of the memories and the damp, muddy leaves I had to sleep on too many nights kept me from that place. I wanted to knock on the door and tell her that I loved her, above all people I loved her: but the memories of the walk of the weary and the frightened froze my feet; and the terrible feeling of cradling a weakening baby froze my arms; and the desperation of trying to squeeze milk from breasts that were themselves undernourished froze my heart.

It was after days and days of uncertain walking. We didn't know what the outcome would be. We didn't know where we were really heading or why we were really walking. We just knew we had to be hidden. Couldn't be found. Had to keep the children away. Mustn't let them get to us. And why? Because we were who we were. Because of our eagle-hearted ancestors and the red flag of our lips and the soft, shy utterances of our mouths. Because we dared to bring more Shqiptar children to life, because we wanted our words to be recognised. Not adored or venerated or made higher than any others. But just to count, just to matter, just to be able to sing our old songs and tell our old stories and to exist. Just to exist.

I was grumpy, I admit it. My arms were weighing down, carrying the child I had borne only two months before. I cursed his birth, although I knew that really I was cursing them, those who had caused this misery. 'Why bring a child into this bitter world?' I said to my husband. 'To be hunted and hated and dispersed and despised. The agony of birth to be confronted so soon with the agony of death?' I had given up. I sat in the mud and I refused to go on. 'Let them catch me,' I said. 'I want a chance to scratch my nails down one of their hard faces,' I said. 'I will dig into their skin so deeply and stare into their eyes and ask them why a child, so small and unknowing, should be subjected to this.'

'You're tired,' my husband said. 'You need a rest. Let me carry the baby. You go on with the others and I'll walk slower behind you all.' I hadn't told him about the milk flow beginning to change.

I had tried to feed the baby that morning and he'd screamed, demanding more, as the white liquid, thin and watery, dribbled from my nipple. He'd sucked and sucked but the flow was so small, a pathetic attempt at nourishment, and he'd created a scene. And I couldn't blame him. But bread and biscuits and the jarred peppers hadn't lasted very long and although the others gave me what they could from their rations, my body was beginning to rebel.

'He's hungry,' I said. 'The milk isn't coming so much. I'm not eating enough and I can't keep feeding him on nothing. I'm worried that soon it will dry up and he'll die, just like his brother did before.'

My husband is a serious man. He did not try to make me feel better or say that this was not the case. But he called the other children and his brother and his wife and his uncle and his aunt and he explained the situation to them all. 'We must give,' he told our own small ones quietly. 'For the baby, we must give. And you will be hungry tonight. And you may be hungry tomorrow. But we will find help and we will not be hungry forever. Give your food to your mother.' They did so, little angels, and although their mouths told me differently, they were happy to keep their tiniest brother alive. And although each mouthful tasted of guilt, I knew that this must happen.

Sleeping under the trees, covered in plastic sheets that would frost each morning, I wondered if we would have to sacrifice this little one for them all. *You're going crazy*, my mind told me. But these situations and this terror and the walking, the walking, the walking, made me think in these unnatural turns. I almost laughed when I thought of the hundreds of German marks we had, ready to bribe the soldiers, but nowhere to spend it and no food to buy. What a ridiculous situation we found ourselves in.

Before I awoke, my husband and his brother had searched

the area. A house, not far away. But were they friends or enemies? Did they want us alive or dead? And would their cow, stood promisingly in the garden, have milk for a family and for a little soul not yet comfortable in the world enough to know if it would stay or not?

'I think that I should go,' I said. 'They will listen to a woman. Even if they are enemies, surely the hardest heart cannot ignore a mother's pleas to keep her child alive?' I knew that this was not the case, but I didn't want my husband or his brother to be seen, knowing that they were particularly after the men.

As I knocked on the door, I felt such relief. I could hear the sweet sounds of Albanian being spoken and then this face, the one now so worn and so silent, was there and she was saying that yes they did have a cow and that yes, it produced good milk and then no, no they would not sell it to me.

They wouldn't sell the milk to me.

They wouldn't sell the milk.

My baby cawed a little in my arms.

'I will give you milk. There will be no charge. And what else do you need? You must come in and rest.'

We didn't know this woman but we huddled into her sitting room and she gave us bread and tea and milk and peppers. She gave us warmth and comfort and peace and hope. Even if only for a short time.

'Why are you not heading on further?' my husband asked. 'They may come here. They may find you.'

'We are too old for running,' said her husband. 'If they come, they come. God will decide. We have sent away our family and we pray each day for their safe return.'

We stayed there three nights. It was hard to leave. Milk

each day, the warmth of walls, a cow to cheer up the little ones, bread, tea, kindness. It was hard to leave.

It wasn't too long after that, when the liberators came. We'd made it to a higher village and we stayed in the barns and houses as trucks rolled into town. Arrivals from yesterday told us that the liberators were coming. But, of course, we couldn't trust. We had undone all the years of trust that life had taught us in just a few short weeks.

But the UN sign on the side of the vehicles told us this was true. And we went into the streets, every one of us. Probably three thousand people in that tiny village and we all went outside and the children had no idea what was going on. But they could see that we were happy, for the first time in months. 'Are we going to stop walking now, Mama?' one of my smallest asked me.

'Yes,' I replied. 'No more walking.'

'Ne jemi të lire,' we shouted. We shook hands with men who didn't speak our language. We touched our hearts. We shed tears, of course. We sang our songs. The children gazed adoringly at the khaki trucks and these people who had come from places they'd never seen, to save us.

And I held our baby aloft and I said a silent prayer and I thanked that man and that woman aloud, even if I was only talking to the sky, and I asked God to bless them and I blessed them myself and thanked them again and again and again.

I held our baby aloft. High. In the air. My precious trophy of survival.

How to Leave a Kosovan Husband

THINKS SHE SHOULD say it. Wants to say it. Musters up the courage. Can't. Will leave it for another day. Will do it though. She will do it.

Another day comes. Puts it off. Not today. Not the right time.

And then there is never the right day. There is never the right time.

So she just blurts it out.

'I think I should leave. I want to leave. I need to leave. I know you are a good husband but I just don't want to stay.'

There. She has said it.

The Maiden in the Box

T HE DAUGHTER OF the king and the boy's mother
lived happily side by side. The mother was so happy. She
had food, she had company and one day soon, she hoped that
she would have her son back where he belonged. The daughter
of the king and the mother lived together and worked together
in the house. They laughed and told stories and both women
became more beautiful, because they were full of joy and
because they had something to look forward to.

There were many men who made a living selling things
in their town. One day, one of these men knocked on the
woman's door and tried to sell the woman and the king's
daughter metal items. They did not want to buy but when
the trader saw the king's daughter he wanted to have her. He
wanted her to be his wife. Every day he knocked on their door
and every day she told him that she did not want to buy and
she went to the back of the house to hide, for she knew that
this man was trying to steal her away. She could tell by his
flashing eyes and his simpering smile. She could tell by his
flattering words and his slippery hands. No matter what she
said, he did not give up. He sent other people to speak to her
about him but she always told them that she was married and
that he should leave her alone.

The man was jealous and unhappy and so he wrote a
wicked letter to her husband.

How to Become a Kosovan Writer

HER LECTURER TELLS her that writers just write. 'No big secret, no special ingredients,' she laughs. 'The secret is just to write. Every day. Just to write.'

And so she does. On a Sunday, in her town. She gets up early, before the whole family is awake. Sometimes the stars are still there when she goes downstairs to feed the dog first thing. And on these days, before she writes a word, she just stares at the stars. She cannot believe that what they say about the stars is true. She feels it is too much to imagine, the huge universe out there, her tiny life, why things happen and where it will all go.

And then she goes to the lounge and takes out some pancakes that her mother has made in the week and she spreads them with ajvar. And then she rolls them and she eats them whilst she starts to write in her notebook. She writes, and when her mother gets up she makes her coffee and she tells her off for working and eating at the same time. And the Returned Girl writes for three hours. Mixing up the stories, changing around the characters, but still trying to retain the essence of truth. And then, in the afternoon, she visits neighbours, friends, relatives: anyone who will tell her a story.

'You don't have enough university work to do?' her father says.

'You will upset people,' her mother says. 'It is not good to bring back the past.'

But still she writes.

The Woman Who Left
Her Children to Die

YES, YES SHE did. Left them to die by some rocks on a hill. *What kind of a mother does that?* I hear you say. *What mother will leave her own children to fend for themselves, lonely and frightened and hungry and available for the soldiers to get to? What kind of mother will carry on walking herself and leave three little innocents to the mercies of the steadily darkening world?*

I will tell you. She is tired. Her husband is in Sweden. He lives there and works there and comes back when he can. It is difficult. The country is controlled so much and he finds it harder and harder to return. But he is making more money than he ever can at home. And they cannot join him, would not be allowed, aren't considered trustworthy enough for such privileges.

And then all this happened. And they had to go. And she spoke to her husband on the telephone just five days before and she said that this might happen and she wept. She wanted him with her so badly.

And he, in Sweden, on the end of a telephone, sick with fear about his wife and their precious children, not to mention the aunts and the uncles and the mothers and the fathers and the cousins and the friends and the neighbours. He can do nothing and he grips the telephone, as if by gripping it so hard he can make any sort of difference. But he cannot.

And he goes to the government offices the next day and tells them that his wife and children are living in occupation. And they will be killed, slaughtered, murdered, raped, hunted, lost, lost forever. But he sees in their eyes a kind of disbelief and they know so little about his country and tell him to trust Bill Clinton, the man in the grey suit so far away. *But his wife. But his children.* He sits all day on a bench in the street. He does not know what to do.

And then, back at home. His wife is, of course, surrounded by family, by neighbours and friends. But she must do all the thinking. She must do all the preparing. She must do all the carrying and the chiding and the cajoling that involves taking three young children on such a journey.

And they walk and they walk and they walk and they walk. And they cry and they cry and they cry and they cry. And they're hungry, so hungry, so hungry, just so hungry. And they all want Mama to carry them. And they all want Mama to kiss them. And they all want Mama to talk to them and to remain cheerful and to keep them going.

And then something inside her breaks. And she can't. Won't. Can't.

She leaves them. Puts them down. Tells them to stay. And she walks.

Of course, there are neighbours around her, but they have their own children to carry. And they must take sacks of flour for bread and tools and blankets. They want to help but they cannot.

There is a boy. Not yet eighteen. Not married. No children. And he stops and he says he will carry two of them.

And he gives her some bread and tells her to rest for a while. In his mind he wants to take a knife to the soldiers who have turned this woman into *this* woman. He knows her. She is a neighbour and he sees in her face the far-away husband and the cries of the children and the worry and the solitary decision making and he knows that he must help to keep the children alive.

He gets her up and he hands her the smallest. And he picks up the other two and carries them on each shoulder. They are a strange carnival of desperation.

So the children do not die. And she does not leave them. But she did. And she would have done. For that is what this world can do to you, when horror is unleashed.

A Baby Left in the Woods

I DIDN'T SEE them myself, but I heard from others that this happened. Another tiny life to take on or to abandon. Do you step over the child, hardening your heart, or do you think of the mother, clearly wild with fatigue, and try to save her from later, right-minded grief? Do you become like them and think that one more life does not really matter or do you share your food a little more thinly and tell your own children that there is no more bread?

The little life reddens and twists and cries.

You make your decision.

How to Leave a Kosovan Husband

H E IS CALMER now.

'You can go,' he says, 'but the children will stay with me. That is right, that is correct, that is traditional.'

He has trapped her again.

Think of his dishonour, if you go, she says to herself. *That is why he wants them.* And he does love them. And he does love them, of course, she sees that.

She watches her little boy playing on the floor. He is beginning to sound out the letters in reading books and she loves to hear him making up stories whilst looking at the images. She likes the pictures he draws of her, of him, of his sister, of her husband, of the trees and the birds and the flowers.

And the little girl who has learnt to say *Mami* and who curls in her lap and plays with her hair.

'And where will you live?' he says. 'You have no house and no job.'

'And what will you say to your family?' he says.

'And what will you say to my family?' he says.

'What is your reason? There is no reason.'

She cannot leave. She knows she cannot leave. She does not know why she said it. She does not know why she uttered the words.

The Maiden in the Box

T HE BOY OPENED a yellow envelope that had travelled far across the sea. In it were lies and wickedness and trouble and deceit. The trader had written to the boy and had told him that his wife was secretly allowing men into her house, without his mother's knowledge. *She does not love you,* the letter said, *she is spreading her love far and wide and she has forgotten her husband completely.*

The boy was so upset and angry and shocked that he ran to the docks and boarded a boat home, without even saying goodbye to his Godfather. The whole journey he raged and boiled with anger. He was working so hard to try to get enough money for a home and a new life together; how could she repay him like this?

When he stepped off the boat, he ran all the way to his mother's house. His wife was looking out of her window and she saw him coming and ran out to him and kissed him and flung her arms around him. 'The most wonderful surprise,' she called out to him, 'to see you again. Why didn't you tell us you were coming?'

Without even speaking to her or asking her if what the letter said was true, he grabbed her around the neck, so tightly that he marked her unblemished skin, and he dragged her through the streets whilst she cried and he threw her violently into a nearby river. He did not think of her at all. He thought of his pride and his honour and his dignity. He did not think at all. He just felt jealousy and anger and sickness and betrayal.

He then went into his mother's house and spoke to his mother. His mother could hardly speak. She was so shocked at what she had just seen and so ashamed that her son could act so rashly and so foolishly. His mother told him that this man was not good and had tried each day to win over his wife, but that she had always stayed away from him and she had always been faithful. 'And now you have thrown away the most precious thing you ever possessed,' said his mother. 'You foolish boy. You stupid boy. You wicked, wicked boy.'

How to Be Part of a
Kosovan Political Party

THEY MEET EARLY on a Friday evening and three of them have brought the paint. There is a sense of hope about them tonight. There is a sense of fear about them tonight. There is a sense of vitality about them tonight.

They can hear each other's footsteps echoing on the concrete as they walk. They say nothing. They don't need words.

They find the billboard and whilst three of them keep watch, the others climb and spray. Big, sprawling, bold letters appear across those signs. This is why she loves this party. Words matter, slogans matter, what you say matters and they want to get their message out there.

As she holds on to the spray can she can feel the energy spurt out onto the billboard. It is red, of course, blood red. Because blood matters. And they want to remind anyone who sees this of the colour of the flag they want and of the spilling of blood by the people they want to reject.

And she is now spilling the paint, her blood, onto the big white canvas. *I have become a writer tonight, an artist tonight. Tonight there is blood.*

The Little Boy Who Danced

THE SOLDIER IS drunk. He's bored out of his brains standing on this road, watching this endless parade of people carrying blankets and children and bread. After a bottle or two, they look like small walking woollen mountains in a variety of colours: that offensive red, that shy grey, that tired muddy brown.

He can't help it. When he gets drunk, he gets happier. And louder. It is part of what happens.

At least I am not aggressive when I am drunk, he says to himself, laughing at the walking blankets parading past him. It is almost like a ridiculous fashion show, he thinks to himself as he wolf-whistles at a model.

'Shame on you,' a woman says.

He just laughs. It isn't him, it is just the way he gets when he's been drinking. He knows this is a serious situation, but the drink makes him laugh. Every time.

And then he sees a little boy, a wavering mass of bag and coat and tiredness. He loves little children. They are so sweet and surprising and always cheer him up. His own little sister dances at family parties and he has a strange sickening longing in his stomach to be at one of those gatherings right now, with his mother's home-made bread and that safe, solid feeling all around.

'Put down your bags,' he says, as the little boy begins to quiver. 'Don't worry, I'm not going to hurt you. I like children.'

The little boy looks at his mother. She stares at the soldier but her mouth will not move. She does not look angry, more like she is concentrating very hard. And then she stares at her son and prays with her whole heart that this will not be the last glance. She stares at his gaunt little face, his worried little eyes, his sad little feet.

'I want to see you dance,' the soldier says.

The boy just looks at him.

'Dance,' the soldier says.

'But, there isn't any music,' says the little boy, his eyes wide with fear.

'I want to see you dance.' This is getting annoying. Can't the boy understand that he is bored and drunk and just wants entertainment? Why doesn't he just do what he's told?

'You're shouting. I'm scared,' says the little boy, a stray tear running down his cheek.

The soldier knows he is not shouting. He knows that if he shouted, he would sound ten times louder. His voice would rattle with rage to the end of the line and back again. He would burst the ear drums of the entire world. He is just loud and drunk and half numb, half heartbroken.

'Please dance for me, little boy,' he tries to whisper but half sneers.

The little boy should be at school parties. He should be at weddings and family occasions. He should be with his friends, messing about on the way home from football. He should be arguing with his sister and messing up the vegetable patch with his running around.

The little boy is dancing. Kicking his legs, with tears streaming down his face, to silent music. He bends and twists his arms, the way he has seen his father and his uncle do at a family party. In his head he is counting the beat of the bold Albanian music, the only thing that will keep out the humiliation he is feeling. In his heart he is feeling the rhythm of the bold Albanian music, the only thing that will stop the strong desire that is building up inside him to run his little boy fists into that ridiculous face and those stupid, pathetic, drunken eyes.

Around him people start to stare and then to laugh and then the whole line, about two hundred people, is laughing, because it is so funny to see a small boy dancing to no music, with no home and no reason to dance. They laugh until they put down their bags and their blankets and until they hold their sides and have to wipe the tears from their worn-out faces.

As they laugh, he picks up the pace and exaggerates the movements. He swoops an arm here and exaggerates a flick of a leg there. Soon everyone is watching and he is running out of breath, performing this strange, bird-like, twisting dance.

'Keep walking,' the soldier says, slurring the ends of his words. 'And stop dancing. You look like a fool,' he shouts, his mirth turned to loathing turned to hatred. He picks up another bottle and pushes down the memory of his own little sister with another swig.

How to Leave a Kosovan Husband

T HERE IS NO choice but to stay, if she wants her children. And she wants her children.

And there could be more. He still climbs onto her, at night. He says, whilst opening her up, that this is her duty. And she does not even protest, because she knows that he thinks that it is. And she knows that they think that it is too. So, it isn't even against her will, because there is no will left any more. This is all part of the deadening. And she's not even there. She's not even in the room whilst he's doing it. Because she's elsewhere, somewhere, thinking of swimming.

She's swimming with all three children. The one who died too. And they're all surrounded by protective water, as if that will save them. As if that will bring them home. And she's floating, floating out to sea. Her body's swollen with water and her lips are blue, but she's suddenly happy, because she can feel nothing. She feels nothing.

The Maiden in the Box

THE BOY WAS overcome with grief. *What had he done? Why had he acted so hastily? Why had he ruined the most valuable thing in his life?*

The boy ran to the river and searched for his wife, or the body of his wife, or any remainder of her, but he could find nothing. He gathered a group of people and they searched and searched. They looked to see if she had been swept up on the riverbanks or if she was floating downstream or if she had managed to cling to an overhanging tree by the side of the river, but the boy's wife was not there. There was no trace of her at all.

The boy, overtaken with emotion, ran deep into the hills.

How to Find a Kosovan Boyfriend

T HEY'VE DONE IT. Their first piece of graffiti for the party. And it feels like nothing she has ever felt before. She feels the most powerful she has ever felt. Like she has done something. Like she could do something.

They run, scatter into the evening, laughing, and he's right next to her. Their hands brush as she passes the paint back to him and he puts it in his backpack and they then find a bar to go and wash their hands. She feels like Lady Macbeth, from the play they've been looking at in lectures. 'A little water clears us of this deed,' she says out loud and the other girls in the bathroom stare at her, as if she's a madwoman, talking to herself. But she doesn't care. But she doesn't care.

And there he is, waiting outside for her. He's so different to all the other men she sees in the street. They all wear jeans and T-shirts with slogans emblazoned across their chests. He looks old fashioned: he's got a long coat and a scarf like Rugova and she wishes she could melt into his serious face.

And off they walk, past the statues, past the stands selling sunglasses, past the sunflower seed stalls and up to the library, which she loves, which she hates. It is like a city, each separate box with the little roof that looks like a plis, and within these boxes, to her, is the world. There is so much to read, there is so much to know. But then the knowing reminds her of all that there is to know and all she can never know. But then the knowing reminds her of where she is and where she cannot go.

She spoke to her father about going to study abroad when she had finished university and he said, kindly but plainly, that he did not want her to be disappointed and so he was going to tell her that the answer was always going to be no. Because of money. Because of visas. Because they might not even recognise her degree abroad. And because, and this was the biggest because of all, they didn't want to lose her. Allow her to go and then never see her back.

But she doesn't want to think of that now. She pushes these thoughts to the back, away, and focuses on this tiny moment of life and promises herself she will make the most of it.

They sit on one of the steps in the dark and he pulls her close to him and she feels his heart beating extra fast and she thinks, *he is nervous too, he is nervous too*. And they must be careful to stay hidden because there could be relatives or neighbours walking by. This is the unspoken thing they both know. And they sit for an hour, in silence, just staying as close as they can to each other. She breathes in every moment. *This is what it is to be alive*, she thinks. *This is what it is to be alive.*

The Lists

What to take:
Jars of peppers
Biscuits
Pocketfuls of bread
Bags of flour
Bottles of water
Sheets of plastic
Blankets
As many clothes as we can wear
Painkillers
Bandages
Photographs of Grandmother and Grandfather
Three gold rings
German marks
As much hope as we can muster

Seen:
A village
Five cows
Four goats
Three mountains
A forest of trees
Thousands of people
A city of tears
Three dead bodies

One baby left for dead in the woods

Food that is left:
Two pocketfuls of stale bread
One jar of flour
A small bag of salt
Two bottles of water

Counted:
Twenty-six nights
Two villages
One night in a tractor
Three nights in a garden
Seven nights in a barn
Hundreds of hand grenades
Thousands of gun shots
Millions watching on TV screens
60, 000 people walking
Two parents, beside themselves with worry
One uncle, worn out, despairing
One frightened little girl

What is left:
One burned house
Eight dead chickens
Bedsheets, muddy and strewn about the house
Four rooms of blackened furniture
The remains of several weeks of meals, spread carelessly
around the kitchen
Four old photographs of the family, ripped at the edges but
still recognisable (Thank God! Thank God!)

School books, scattered on the floor, but still in good condition

The little girl's toy doll

One bag of memories, buried safely in the garden

A note, scribbled, left under the broken door

How to Leave a Kosovan Husband

S O, HE GOES to work and she takes just a few things for each of them and then they are on a bus, trundling through the landscape. She is staring out of the window at the cows in gardens attached by rope to the orange brick houses and the chickens, roaming free in the sun. There are loads of children out to play and she sees their reckless abandon and she wishes to be them. She wishes to be cut loose, free of knowing, free of knowing.

'Where are we going, Mummy?' the little boy asks.

'Just on holiday,' she replies.

'Without Daddy?'

'Yes, without Daddy this time.'

She swallows back the guilt and they eat their bread and cheese and she tries to make her plans, think of somewhere they can stay, think of how she can make very little stretch as far as a few towns away at least.

They get there by mid-afternoon and it is deadly cold. She can feel the cold in her own fingers and knows it must be biting at her children even more. She carries the little girl, keeps her wrapped up, close, protected. The little boy is doing well, trotting beside her and keeping up, asking the endless questions.

She finds a place to stay, a small room that a man says he will give her for a week for the money she has left.

Just one step at a time, she tells herself. *Don't think about the next step, just this one, and then the next will come to you.* That's what they did in the mountains when she was a girl. That's what her mother told her kept them going. *And they survived,* she tells herself. *They made it through.*

The room is tiled on the floor, cold and slippery. They will all sleep in one large bed which has three blankets over a quilt and is still not warm enough.

At the time he gets in from work, the text messages start:
Where are you?
Where have you gone?
Why aren't you here?
I called your mother and you aren't there, where have you gone?
Answer me
If you have taken my children . . .
Tell me where you are
Answer my calls. Don't ignore me.
And then they stop for an hour. And then they start again:
You forget that I know where your family are
If you don't answer me, you know I will hurt them
You know I will do what it takes to get my children back
Remember the Kanun
Remember that I will not be dishonoured.

The Maiden in the Box

WHAT NOBODY KNEW was that, when the girl
had been thrown into the river by her hasty husband,
some fishermen had been standing by the river trying to catch
fish and not really having much luck. When they saw the
girl floating by, icy and bloated, they threw out their nets,
caught her, and pulled her to the side of the river. She was
nearly drowned, all blue and cold and frozen, having been
surrounded by water for so long, but they wrapped her in a
thick cloak to try to revive her.

A man came by to buy fish for his supper but the fishermen told him that they had caught nothing but a woman
that day. When the man saw the woman, he felt like his heart
would explode with desire. He saw that she was beautiful and
that she had a face so brave it almost made him frightened.
He knew that he wanted to have the woman for himself. He
offered the fishermen five thousand lek for her. 'She's probably
dead, anyway,' said the fishermen to each other. 'What harm
will it do if we sell her to him? And we have caught no fish
to sell today.' So the fishermen sold the woman to the man
and he took her away.

When she awoke the woman was frightened, although she
did not show it, because the river had not only frozen her
body. She lay there, inspecting this strange man with rough
hands and a rough beard and probably rough intentions too,
she thought. *I am like a giant fish, cold and caught and clammy,*

she thought. She moved her feet and they flapped about and floundered. She moved her arms and she struggled to make them move and come back to life. *Any man who will buy a frozen woman is not to be trusted*, she thought. She needed a plan.

The man was now looking at her and he could clearly see that she was reviving. He began to stroke her wet, cold face. He ran his hands along her bluish pink legs. He kissed her lost, pale cheek. 'Now you belong to me,' he said. 'You are mine and I will keep you with me on my journey.' The woman began to shiver violently. 'You're still so cold, beautiful one,' the man said. He wrapped her in a blanket so tightly she could hardly breathe.

When she was warmer, she began to speak, soft little shivery words at first and then she regained her voice and she spoke in bold and decisive tones. She told the man that along the road there were many dangerous men and that if they saw her with him, they would take her away. 'Let me dress in some of your clothes and pretend to be a man,' she said, 'then you will be able to keep me.'

The man thought that this was a good idea and he was amazed by the woman's quick thinking, for he knew that she was beautiful but he did not expect her to be clever. He gave her some clothes and she went to change behind a bush. The man's horse was grazing near to the bush and she gently called him over to her. When the horse was near, she grabbed his reins and rode him far away, as fast as she could. The man was left with nothing.

How to Have a Kosovan Boyfriend

THEY MUST ALWAYS be careful to avoid relatives and neighbours. Not because they are ashamed, not because they are ashamed. But the freedom. The freedom is to be kept for as long as possible. Before the questions and the demands and the introductions. Before the hints and the contracts and the expectations.

'Let us have three months,' he says, 'before we tell anyone.'

'Let us have a lifetime,' she says, 'before we tell anyone.'

They make plans, as if they are another European couple, to travel around Europe and to make a living in England. Of course, this will never happen. Of course, this will never happen. But the maps and the guidebooks and the fantasies are part of the joy. They plan the journeys they will never take; they choose restaurants they will never sit in; they look at pictures of beds in hotel rooms where they will never lay their heads, never curl up close, never kiss each other's faces and in which they will never talk about their lovely days of sightseeing and eating and chasing pigeons in famous squares.

He has an apartment in Pristina which he shares with his older brother and his older brother's wife. But they are away most weekends and she manages to tell her father that she is staying in Pristina to study one weekend. And she manages to tell her aunt that she will visit a friend this same weekend.

And they must enter the apartment block separately, of course. And he must buy them food for the whole weekend, of course. And they must not let anyone hear a girl's voice there, of course.

She closes her eyes and strokes his arm and then his face and then his chest. 'What are you doing?' he says. 'You don't want to look at me?'

And she says that yes, of course, she does, she does, of course, but that she is imagining being a sculptor and she is imagining that she must make a sculpture of his body and she must remember it so well with her hands so that she can recreate it later. 'It will be bronze and tall and shining and I will place it on Mother Teresa Avenue, so that everyone can walk by and see you glinting in the sunshine, radiating yourself to the world like all those who are frozen in time and captured there: the famous leaders and the historical figures and the most selfless and saintly Albanian, Teresa,' she says.

'You are a funny girl,' he says, teasing.

And she becomes quiet and will not speak at all.

And he is sad and says that she is the one who has become a statue and he says, 'Why? Why?' She does not answer. She stays so still, like she is made of stone. She wonders if she really is made of stone.

'How can I wake you up, Hermione?' he says, teasing her from her favourite Shakespeare play.

And then she tells him that she needs to give him her real name. 'I did not give it to you before, but my real name is the Returned Girl,' she says.

She tells him the story of the Returned Girl. He listens, without interrupting. She hangs her head. She does not look him in the eyes.

He lifts her face so that her eyes meet his. 'It is the most beautiful story I have ever heard,' he whispers to her. Then he keeps on whispering as he learns her body. He tells her that he wants to remember it so that he can later make a statue of her. He whispers that she has a new name now: *loved, cherished, newborn.*

The Liberation

THAT NIGHT, THE families sleeping on floors and in barns and under plastic and in tractors actually slept. A chorus of snoring sang out to celebrate the freedom that had come. The breathing was a little deeper that night. The resting was a little more restful that night. The dreaming was a little more hopeful that night. Mothers and fathers felt that they could, for the first time in months, sleep with both eyes closed. They relaxed their grip on their children, just a little. Teenagers let their mothers kiss them before bed time and did not insist on looking embarrassed. Grandparents almost allowed themselves to congratulate themselves on their large families and went through a mental list of who was left. Mothers stirred and touched the foreheads of their children just to make sure that they were real. Fathers woke, hearts pounding, and counted their children over and over. *We did not lose one. Thank God. Thank God.*

Others, less happy, reached out in their sleep for arms that were not there to hold any more. They reached to absence, nothing, absence, memories and still found nothing there. Three children, missing. A grandfather, never seen again. A sister rumoured to have been taken. An injured arm; a painful foot; a battered leg; a mind so full of terror that it couldn't think how to live any more; a face so changed, so damaged, so unrecognisable. Some slept a little. Some woke at every hour. Some were terrorised with distressing dreams of hunters and rabbits caught in traps. The cruellest trick was waking in the morning, forgetting, then remembering as the sun came up to taunt you once again with another day.

That night, women peeled layers of clothing from men. Men used their tongues to explore the soft crevices of wives. And couples, surrounded by family at every corner, found ways to find silent spaces, to silently love each other.

Hands clung to hands, wiped away tears, grabbed at bodies; lips touched lips touched shoulders touched noses touched thighs touched breasts touched freedom. Mouths met mouths, ate each other up as if they were the bread they had been short of for so long. Bodies reminded each other that they could still feel, could still exist, could still remain. Thank God.

Couples, frozen by the nagging worries of war and the daily arguments, resumed a kind of bodily peace. Hands said what speech could not. Eyes said what mouths dared not say. Lips spoke, but not with words.

One young girl, engaged to be married to a local boy, found herself in the arms of a soldier that night. She thanked him for her life in a way that she hadn't known she could. She blocked out what her father had told her about soldiers. She didn't listen to her mother's voice creeping up in the back of her head saying: *dishonour, shame and worthlessness.* Instead she spoke her own words: *gratitude, freedom, life.*

There was ecstasy and tears but mostly relief. Sheer relief. They still had hands and toes and eyes and hearts with which to love the future. They still had arms to re-build houses. They still had noses to smell the pita cooking in the oven. They still had legs with which to walk back home.

One young couple snuck out, too many people in the house they were staying in. They manoeuvred over rows of bodies, sleeping next to each other on the floor, to find a quiet dewy piece of grass on which to be alone to celebrate their bodies and their bones and their hearts and their hands and their salt and their sweat and their smiles and their children still being alive. It was too cold to get fully undressed but they found a way to get as close to each other as possible. They wanted togetherness that night. A cow nudged its way into their celebration and they laughed it away.

A teenage boy found a space alone to deaden the horror of the past days.

Lovers no-one knew about pressed together the tips of fingers or gave each other glances just seconds longer than they should.

And then there are those who had to wait. They could not find a space or their bodies were too weak from eating only bread. Or their minds were elsewhere, re-playing the terrible mental films of fear. They planned to make love when they returned home but their houses were torn down and instead of laying in their bedrooms and joining their bodies, they knelt and cursed and cried, separate in their sorrow.

Others, perhaps more resilient, loved in broken-down buildings. They found romance in broken tables and used their bodies as a prayer to a new world, unbuilt but yet to come.

How to Punish a Kosovan Wife

THE WHOLE JOURNEY in silence. The children are asleep and he says nothing. She even tries to explain, but he does not respond. Nothing. But she can feel his anger in the sharp turns of the steering wheel and the last-minute braking that she hates.

And then, home. The children lifted like sacks of flour into their own beds. And then, in silence, she crawls into her own bed and he, in silence, pins her down and she is punished.

The next day, everything is as it has always been, but he has taken away all the money in the house and he comes back at lunch time and they eat a silent lunch. And, as he leaves, he says that they have the money for the second layer of the house and that they will put it up quickly and that before spring his mother and father will live here too. Above them.

The Maiden in the Box

T HE WOMAN RODE for hours, with the wind through her hair and the horse feeling like the only solid thing in the world. She did not know where she was riding to but she knew that she wanted to be far away from everything.

She had been riding for hours and it was raining and the wind was getting stronger and stronger. It felt as if every gust of wind was determined to push her off the horse. It felt as if the rain would dissolve her so that she too would turn to liquid and become part of it. She could not ride any further. She was tired; she and the horse had to have rest and water. She stopped by the edge of a city. She could go no further and so she found the city gates, so tall and solid amidst this metamorphic weather, and she lay there for the night, exhausted and not knowing what she would do next.

Meanwhile, her father's royal advisors were gathered in a tall building where only the most trusted of men were allowed to enter; they were inside this city with such tall and solid gates and did not know that the king's daughter slept by so closely. They stood around a warming fire whilst the rain battered the stones of the building and the wind made the sound of a woman wailing with grief.

'It must be a sign, this weather,' said one of these men. 'The king, dead, and his daughter nowhere to be found.'

'How will we choose another king?' said another. 'We were relying on the marriage of the princess. Now, what?' They looked at each other seriously, with deep frowns and strong eyes and incredibly troubled hearts.

'We need a fair way to find another king,' said the oldest and wisest of them all. He was a man who held their ultimate respect and they knew that he would find a solution. 'There are many who want this power but wanting power will never give you the ability to hold it well,' he said.

'The next morning we will go to the city gates and find the first man that we see. He will become our king,' said this advisor. The others looked at each other. They were worried and thought that the man was getting old and losing his wisdom.

'We need an ordinary man who has been through many hard things. Humility brings great leadership,' said the old advisor. 'Trust me, I have seen it many times.' He could see that they thought that the plan was not a good one but he knew that what he was saying was true and would lead them to a great ruler.

The advisors were still unsure but this man had been proved over decades to be right about such things. 'We will trust you,' they said, 'and tomorrow we will have a new king.'

How to Break a Kosovan Heart

YOU'RE DRIVING INTO the city and you don't care about the reckless drivers tonight. You're probably more reckless than they are, you think. You're sure you are. It's dark and the lights from the bigger trucks shine right into your face. You nearly go into a wood truck that's travelling too slow. You beep your horn. Again, you beep your horn.

You reach the edge of the city and the traffic is queued up. Just your luck. You need to get to her as soon as you can and whisk her back to the village immediately. And your aunt's apartment is at least six streets away and the traffic is going nowhere. You breathe for the first time in hours. You curse the traffic. You do not know how so many people can have so many cars. You shout to God, out loud, in your car, and you ask him why something cannot go right for you today. You wish that God would cause a giant wind to blow these cars away. So you could just get to her. So you could just get to her.

You're completely still; nothing's moving and so you stare into the streets. You see the women buying shoes and a small boy carrying a large melon, so large it nearly pulls him over. And there are women with headscarves carrying eggs. And then the smarter ones, from the centre of the city, walking home to apartments. And younger university students, thronging back to their homes, some to get on buses back to villages, towns.

And then you spot her. God has listened to you tonight and you say a small prayer to thank him for his answer and you get out of the car and call her over. And she's with a boy, a man, and you don't even care tonight. *Let her be with any boy tonight*, you think. You do not care. It does not matter.

She looks embarrassed, frightened. It must be her boyfriend, but you don't care. You just tell her to get into the car straight away and so she comes, obedient, and she gets in, asks you why you're here and she looks very scared, like you've found out about the boy and you've come to take her away. And you say, 'No, don't worry, I can see he is your boyfriend but that is not why I'm here.'

And she looks relieved. But you don't want that because what you have to say will hurt.

'She's very ill and they don't know if she'll last the night. Maybe a few days at the most. She wants to see you.'

She asks, 'Why didn't anybody know?' And you tell her that you just don't know. You've asked the same questions yourself. And you're getting married in a month and you wanted her there. You can't imagine what it will be like without her. But anyway, your mother wants to see her and you must get her back as soon as you can.

You drive her straight to the local hospital, where your mother is. Your mother looks like she's made of wax. And your sister begins to cry. And your mother begins to cry. And your father, he can't speak.

The Military Hospital

M Y MOTHER RAN a clinic from our house. Always,
she was doing good for people, helping them, trying to
help them to get babies, even if they had given up and they
thought that it was impossible. Even if they had tried and
the babies had turned to a messy bundle of unfulfilled cells
and hopes in their mothers' wombs. She still tried and many
times she was successful, because she listened to their stories
and not just their bodies. And my mother says that calming
a couple can help as much as anything you can do to their
bodies. And she knows these things, my mother. She knows
what to do. And she was able. She was able to help so many
and we were always known as a place who would try for you.
Who would keep on trying and my mother was so loved by
them, even when the trying just turned to sadness. They still
loved her, even then.

So, you can see that that house was special. Was always so.

Of course, everyone loves their own home, especially for
the childhood memories it remembers for you, but our home
was loved by all. And that is why, when it came to the days
we told ourselves would not come; when we were forced to
sleep in our clothes all night; when suspicion turned to fear
turned to warnings turned to leaving: it was particularly hard.
I was a little boy in those days. And when my mother woke
me early in the morning and said that we must go that very
day, that the stories she had told me had come true, I ran to

every wall of the house and kissed it. My little lips pressing the roughness of the tiles, like a flower kissing its own roots.

And then we went through the same as everyone else. The journey and the fear and the hunger and the loss.

But it was coming back that hurt us the most. When the liberators were in town and they had told us we could return. When the lambs no longer needed to fear the wolves. When they told us that we should return to our fold. But when we came back we realised that the danger wasn't over.

Outside our house, a tank. And not one of the friendly ones. And we could see from a few houses away what they had used our house for. It was a military hospital and we were horrified. Not that we wanted anyone dead, not that we wished injury or death or wounds or scars on anyone. No, we were a peaceful family, we wanted only love. But the idea of them using our supplies and our facilities to treat those who had only burned and maimed and terrified our people. That they had experienced healing and we had experienced disease. That they had had plenty of medicine and we had not had enough. That they had used that place of love to fuel those who hated. My mother was sick seven times when she saw it. Right in the road, with neighbours and the UN soldiers watching her. They thought that she was tired and ill, but I knew that it was because of the house.

And there was a dark cloud rising from the house, like some horrible smoke signal, telling us that all was not well and that what we found would twist our insides into rags and that, because they were being forced to go, they would spoil all that they had found and leave it in the opposite way to the way that they had found it, like the rudest and most ungrateful house guests in the world.

So, we couldn't yet get to it. The liberators were with us, so we were confident of safety, but the remains of the enemy were there and the liberators were under orders not to use force unless necessary. There was a huge enemy tank blocking the road and then we saw them. The men in grey, walking out of the house, and they smiled when they saw us, ragged, tired and defenceless, staring at them. One looked right at my mother and said something unthinkable.

My brother was nineteen at the time and he couldn't keep it in. What would you have done if your mother was insulted and your family were sneered at by people who wanted you gone from the earth? He was angry. So angry, his eyes were painful in their sockets. I could see that in his hot stare and in the swift action of his arm and in the pointed fingers that followed the rock that he hurled at a soldier. 'You're the ones who should be dead,' he called at them. 'Not my neighbour and my grandfather and all those men you shot in the hills. You deserve death.'

They didn't know what he said, but they understood anyway. And so did the liberators. And if the liberators hadn't been there then they would have shot my brother dead with the gun that they held out in front of them. As it was, the liberators found it hard to get them not to shoot. But they knew that as soon as they did, the liberators would return their one shot with more than they could manage. They knew that killing my brother would be like killing themselves.

And so they went from our house. Slowly and spitefully, they rolled away in their tanks to the nearby border and they did not get what they deserved but at least we were rid of them.

And so we entered the building, burnt and charred and

spoiled, and as if hate itself had made itself resident. My brother went first, checking each room for traps and grenades, as if they hadn't left us with enough terror already. And, although the sight of it all made my little boy's eyes wide with fear, I knew it was not the fault of the house and that it had been used against its will and that I must kiss each wall again, greeting it and letting it know that we had returned to care for it once more.

We slept there from the first night. We slept in darkness, on floors and under blankets, but it was our own home and we did not want to leave it again. I lay in the space between my mother's arm and her chest and I knew that we would slowly start to make things new in the morning. I knew that my mother would work and work and that we all would work and work until we were bringing new life into the world in this place again. And although I knew our house would never be the same again, I knew that it was still standing and could be repaired.

How to Enlist Some Kosovan Help

S HE COMES TO you, one morning. You don't expect her. She must have walked right through the town, with the children pulling on her arms like pieces of unravelled wool. She raps too loudly at the door and her smile of greeting is too bright, her eyes too wide. And the sweat at the edges of her hair isn't just because the day is so hot. And she has made sure that it is a time when everybody is out, apart from you.

And she gives the children toys to play with. And she shuts the door and says that you must help. And she tells you that it has to end.

And you talk again of honour, of tradition. But she hears in your voice that you don't really mean it. And she says, 'There will be blood. If you don't help, there will be blood.'

You don't know what to say. You see the hot, blue rage in her face and you suggest a holiday, an agreement, some talking to. She says that it won't work.

You see the face has changed from what it was. There's a tiredness about the eyes, an angry tiredness. And there's a gripping of the jaw that wasn't there. And she tells you that she needs your help. And she tells you that she will help herself if you don't help. And she knows that this has got to end. That she has to end it somehow.

You become angry. You ask her why she isn't like the other girls. She doesn't know. She doesn't know. She cries. 'It is more than not being like the others,' she says. It is her fault she thinks, but some of it is not, she is sure of that.

And you tell her that you will go to court. That there may be a chance that court will help. The police can be called. But she says she can't do that. It might not work. There isn't enough time and she can feel herself drowning. And what can she say to the police anyway? What exactly could she say?

And then you say, okay. You will think and plan and there must be some way. There will be some relative she can slip away to, somewhere. But she must leave the children, you say. They cannot go.

'No,' she says, 'they must.'

'They cannot,' you say, 'there will be blood.'

'I cannot leave; I cannot stay,' she says.

'You must make a choice,' you say.

'But you will help me to get them later, perhaps?' she says. 'You will go to court and you will speak for me?'

You say that you will. You feel you owe her that much. You see her submerged little face and know that she will never breathe again unless you promise such a thing. You wince when you realise that even the promise itself has its own weak promise of such unsubstantial results behind it.

The Maiden in the Box

THE NEXT MORNING, after a night of sleep by the city gates, the girl was nearly frozen once again. She could hardly feel her fingers and toes and her horse could hardly move its legs. It was pacing about and whinnying, trying to keep warm. She was surprised it hadn't left her; she was, after all, its very new and demanding master. As she awoke, the king's advisors found her by the gate and, thinking she was a man (for she was still dressed in the man's clothes), they made her the king of the land.

She was given the finest robes to wear and the most succulent dishes to eat. She slept in the comfiest bed, with pillows made of the softest feathers. Nothing was too much trouble.

The people loved their new king. She was kind and wise and ruled them well. At every fountain in Egypt the people placed a picture of their beloved new leader, surrounded by a golden frame. When she heard about this, the king secretly ordered her guards to arrest anyone who spent too long looking at her picture or anyone who sighed when they saw her face. *Those who are captivated by the picture of my face will pay for their past sins*, she thought.

In time, the guards had arrested a tradesman, some fishermen, a man looking for his horse and her husband. They were all brought to the palace, wondering what they had done to displease the King of Egypt. The king did not speak to them immediately and they were left, rotting in the dark jail.

How to Say Goodbye to Your Mother

S HE SITS MEEKLY by the bed and stares. *There was no warning*, she thinks, *it is not fair.*

And her mother says, 'It is better this way, because I will not have to face the trials of old age. And I made it through the war and I know that I got you safely through too,' she says, 'and maybe that is what God's mission for my life was. Maybe I was to save you.'

And she does not like her talking of God, because she does not know where God has been all these years, all her life, all through this darkness. It makes her weep that her mother accepts this fate.

And her mother says she is sorry because she wishes her daughter had never been given the name the Returned Girl. And she wishes she could have spoken up. 'My words have always been actions,' she says. 'I am not strong like you. But now you are speaking and telling our stories and I couldn't be prouder. I couldn't be prouder.'

And her mother looks so grey and fragile, like a statue, ready to be knocked down. And she says, 'But, Mother, you will not speak of the past with me.'

And her mother says, 'Listen, now, and I will begin, before it is too late . . .'

And they stay, for three whole days, in the hospital, talking, and she makes notes. And she hears about their neighbours and their family. And she tells her mother of the new boy and the political party and what she hopes for the future.

'You will do it. I know you will,' her mother says.

Later, her mother slips away, like the daylight changing into the night. Softly, softly, almost as if you hadn't seen it.

The Surprising Children

W E DO NOT talk about these children. You might notice a gleaming head playing with the other children at the edges of the street. You might, if you stood the children up in a line and counted them out for a game of tag or football, notice one who looks a little different. You might catch a face, whilst it was smiling at you, asking for a tomato at a market stall, and think, he has an unusually shaped cheek. But you will say nothing. You are a kind nation and you are a kind, grateful man.

They told the men to go to the hills because they would all be killed if they stayed. You went into those lonely hills, begged by the women in your family to leave as soon as possible. Kushtrim, your brother-in-law, had a small tractor and you and he and three other neighbours used it to get as high as possible and then abandoned it for walking and sleeping behind rocks for three days. You left it three days because you felt that they would have gone by then.

Returning, the horror of what you'd all done strangled you; it tore out your hearts so that they never worked in the same way again. It bit you in the face like a wild dog attacking and then it went for your stomach and your legs and your eyes and your fingers until there really was nothing left.

Kushtrim's wife, dead. His three small children all gone too.

What a relief when you found yours all again. All safe and

still at home. There was even some bread on your arrival. What grateful bliss you felt. You thanked God from the bottom of your heart and physically shook when you thought of the others. You had been spared but their bitter pain was yours.

Your wife, pale but living – she was living, thank God – said that she was well. The children told how they had hidden behind the woodpile in the garden and how mother had stayed in the front of the house, keeping away the soldiers. They told you that they had heard screaming but that none of it, blessedly, was their own. Thank God, thank God for your beautiful wife and children. Thank God. Thank God. Thank God.

It wasn't long before you all had to disappear again. No one would be left again. You wouldn't dare. Those hills, those comforting hills, shielded you again. Thank God.

You couldn't tell Kushtrim about the baby. She showed all the signs and he would soon find out by looking. But his loss, the loss that had turned his thirty-year-old's face into that of a fifty-year-old man's, would not bear the pain of telling. You felt a little guilty that you were allowed more joy.

All your wife and children safe and now one more to add? You wished, almost, that just one of his had been spared in place of this or that you could pass this new one straight to him. But it would be no compensation.

The day of birth was special. Who doesn't love the birth of their child? But after all this murderous fighting, it felt like an extra special miracle. Thank God.

Staring down at his blonde hair and unusual face, you thanked God for him anyway.

A Prayer

O H GOD, WHO sees us all and yet has not moved, I do not understand your ways, but I will trust in you. You made the materials for metal and the mentality of men who murder our people. I am full of rage but I will believe that you are good. You made the soil and the stars and the solid hills that held us safely in their arms. I am full of thanks but I do not understand why we had to run like rats, the rats they said we were. I wonder if you can be good if a man's heart can turn to hatred in this way.

Oh God, forgive me for not telling him. If I had let it out, even a small piece, I would have been broken forever. The cries of birth, only you know, were not cries of pain but the anguish of violation. The cries of birth, violent and shrieking, were cries to you: Oh God, why did this happen? Oh God, where did you go? Oh God, I cannot hold it in any more. Thank God for the birth. The only way of shouting out curses against its reason.

He knows anyway. But if we spoke, if I opened my small, pursed mouth and uttered the story and made it real, we could not bear it. The truth would make us angry beyond bearing and I cannot, will not, let that happen. We can bear it and we will. And it isn't the fault of the innocent. I will not believe that and I will not punish it with my rage.

Oh God, who sees us all and yet has not moved, protect my son. Protect his shining hair and his square jaw and his terrifying beginning. May my people be kind. May they choose blindness over anger. May they choose compassion over hatred and revenge.

How to Say Goodbye to Your Children

S HE HUGS THEM more each evening. Holds them. And
the little boy gets angry, is annoyed, does not want to be
cuddled so much. 'You don't leave me alone, Mummy,' he says.
'I am big now. I don't need cuddles.'

And she gives something to each of them and tells them she
loves them hundreds of times. 'We know Mummy, we know,'
they say and carry on playing.

'And your story is here,' she says, pointing under the bed
at the folder she has managed to hide there. 'This is where I
keep the story I wrote for you and the pictures.'

'We know, Mummy, we know. Why do you keep on telling
us this?'

And she calls you and tells you that she cannot go.

'It is up to you,' you say. 'Your choice.'

And then she calls you again and says she will go. That
after the neighbour's wedding you must take her to the airport.

And again, she calls and says, no.

And again, she calls and says, yes she will.

And you say to her that she must just pack what she needs
and take it to the wedding and then she can decide at the last
moment. 'I will not tell you what to do again,' you say. 'You
must be the one to decide.'

The Maiden in the Box

THE GIRL WHO was the king ordered her guards to bring the prisoners to the palace. 'Tell them that I will pass sentence on all of them today,' she said. The guards were mystified by her orders but they had learned to trust her and so they did what she said without question.

She lined up all the men who had ever wanted to have her and to own her and to decide what she must do and she told them that they must not speak unless she commanded them to do so. 'If you utter a word,' she said, 'that word will be your last.'

Firstly, she asked the tradesman why he had stared and sighed at the picture. And he said that the picture was a picture of a girl he had been in love with, but that he had done many things wrong and had written a letter to the girl's husband saying that she had been unfaithful. He had wanted to cause trouble. He was angry that he couldn't have the girl and he admitted that he wanted to spoil her happiness too.

At this, the girl's husband rose to his feet and tried to strike down the tradesman in anger, but the guards stopped him, just in time.

She then asked the fishermen why they had sighed when staring at the picture. And they said that it was because they had rescued the girl in the picture but that they had made a bad judgement and had then sold her to another man. They admitted that when they should have shown kindness and pity to the girl, they instead had used her to make money.

And then she asked the man who was looking for his horse why he had stared at the picture. And he said that he had bought the girl from the fishermen because he had thought that she was so beautiful and because he had wanted to possess her, but she had run away from him, taking his horse and his clothes.

And then she spoke finally to her husband (who was holding his heart, as if in pain) and asked him why he had sighed. And he said, with tears in his eyes, 'I am the most miserable man in the world. I had the beautiful woman in the picture as my precious wife and then I lost her. And it is my fault, because I did not treat her as I should have done. I believed some terrible things about her and I did not stop to listen to her and find out if they were true.'

And the king looked sad and serious and lost and found all at the same time and then she spoke in solemn tones and said, 'What you have all said is true, indeed.'

How to Send Off a Manuscript

S HE PRINTS IT off at university. She writes her name on the front cover, in blue pen with swirling writing. She reads it another four times and then, with trembling hands, she posts it off.

She feels as if she has posted thousands of lives out into the world and she prays that there will be ears soft enough to listen.

They walk to the coffee shop and she talks to him about her next pieces. She has written about the past; she must now write about the present, try to change it. 'My mother may have saved me for this,' she says. He nods, he buys her coffee, he doesn't say a lot.

The Burning Churches

SOMEWHERE, JUST OVER the border, they torch your place of worship, your house of God, your point of spiritual reference.

Where the pointed spire stretched to the sky to reach to God, where the painter layered golden paint, where the prayers were said over your child and your grandfather and your own small body years ago. Now the gold comes from the flames and they overtake each section of the church, flickering and gorging and greedily eating up each metal cross, each delicate page of holy book, each wooden seat where petitions were made and remorse was felt and where families, squashed together, came to worship.

The heat begins to overwhelm the room and candles lie in hot melted puddles, boiling and simmering. The smell of incense overtakes as the church becomes a giant prayer to the world: *let there be an end to this, let there be an end to this, let there be an end.*

The Burning Mosques

SOMEWHERE, JUST OVER the border, they torch your place of worship, your house of God, your point of spiritual reference.

Where the slender minaret stretched to the sky to reach to God, where the builder placed each careful brick to make the detailed domed ceiling, where the prayers were said and peace was desired for your child and your grandfather and your own small body years ago. Now the desire comes from the flames and they overtake each section of the mosque, flickering and gorging and greedily eating up each silver tap, each delicate page of holy book, each embroidered mat where petitions were made and remorse was felt and where, side by side, families came to worship.

The heat begins to overwhelm the room and the calligraphy on the walls starts to peel away, shrivelling and retreating. The smell of burning overtakes as the letters become cinders and the mosque becomes a giant prayer to the world: *let there be an end to this, let there be an end to this, let there be an end.*

Monuments and Statues

FIRST, THEY START with the head and batter it down, until it crashes onto the street to a cacophony of cheers. The stone splits open as if an invisible knife has sliced it in two. They believe that it is God's invisible hand, God's invisible knife.

And then there is the body, the body of the man who is a hero in some other minds. Some minds far away, some minds separated from these angry ones. And the body will not move, no matter how they rock, how they smash and shove and shake.

One man has an idea. He has a cousin, with a digger, and he will call him and get him to bring it to the town centre. And now this man has had his hand shaken by all the other men. He is to be respected, he is to be thanked, he really is the hero. The man is pleased, reddened by the attention. He really must buy his cousin a box of cigarettes for all the honour the promise of his digger has brought him.

And now a crowd has gathered. Older men bring their sons and grandsons to watch. They lecture of their history, their language, the respect to be afforded their inheritance. 'This is what you call an education,' they say. 'This is what you should be doing,' they say. 'Not wasting your time on those mindless video games which teach you nothing.' Some of these men are doctors, teachers, lawyers. *Not what you'd call vandals. Not what you'd call vandals.*

The digger has arrived to whistles and shouts and cheers. They all record this on their phones. This needs to be remembered. This needs to be shown to the whole family. It is more watchable than the wedding videos their wives play over and over and over.

The monument is not going down without a fight. It stands, proud, for three separate blows. 'That's because they made it with metal they stole from us,' they say. 'No wonder it is strong.'

And there it goes at last, toppling to the sound of great applause. The destruction is so wonderful, the anger is so raw, the power is so palpable. Each man runs in to kick the rubble, hurting his feet and bolstering his pride. One man takes a picture of himself with the grounded statue and then they all join in. Who wouldn't be proud of being there on this great day? Anyone who is anyone would take part.

Eventually they dissipate. Back to their homes and their wives and their coffee shops and, mainly, their unemployment.

The monument lies in the town centre, its ruin stirring hatred in other hearts far away.

The Man in the Coffee Shop

A H, HOW THEY love to go to coffee shops, these men. Say, they work in the municipality; perhaps they are in charge of culture or sport or education, or maybe they have an administration role or they are in charge of the local police force; part of this role is to visit the coffee shops each day. They must do it. It is to be expected.

The Minister for Culture, shall we say? Round, with a bulbous nose and a stomach that bloats like a watermelon over his trousers – the very smartest of cheapest of costly trousers – will think nothing of spending five out of six hours of his working day in a coffee shop. He must meet the other important men in town. They must have long, loud, thundering conversations about this detail or that detail. About how it was done in the old days. About what would be done in Albania. About what is respectful and right. They will talk and talk and talk and talk and talk. They will not mention the money that never makes its way to the schools or the cultural centre. They will not mention the fact that they are being paid for these conversations. They will not think it strange that the people who take part in these meetings in coffee shops all look the same. It is all part of their role. It is to be expected.

The Minister for Culture will take a long, slow puff of his cigarette. He absorbs so much smoke all day that the thick crust of his skin is becoming slightly yellow and his pores seem to have opened up; they have given up trying to stop the poison coming in. He has a bristly moustache over his mouth – it is so thick and rough that his grandchildren whisper that he has a brush on his face. The war has taken away his genuine smile, but instead of the sensitivity that is found in so many of these delicate people, he has allowed a thick, sludgy laziness to boil up in his stomach. He talks seriously, all day long, and says that he cares about this or about that issue, but really, he feels nothing. He is a round plastic bucket of a man; he has the potential to be useful, but really he is empty.

He promises people that he will do this or he will do that. The anguished young teenagers from the local school who ask him about putting on an exhibition. Or the earnest teacher of art from a nearby village who asks about some extra supplies. 'Of course,' he tells them, 'we can arrange this or that such a thing.' But he will never do it. He knows, even as he utters the words, that he will never fulfil their meaning.

How can such a man live with himself? How can he take his wages for such a job?

He is not the only one. They all know that as soon as another political party comes to power, their wages will stop and they will be thrown out. It is like he is a man on death row, waiting to die and putting up no resistance to save himself. *What is the point?* he might say to himself. *I am feeding my family for now. Thank God I have this job for now. We are living, we are not dying.*

Stooping over his qaj i Rusit, his Russian tea, made extra strong because he is a man, an important man, he opens another packet of sugar and stirs it in. He is not the kind of man to consider his days; he just gets through them now. He knows the regular signposts: the tea, the cigarettes, the document he might sign, the visits, the coffee, the drive for five minutes to get to his home at the other end of the street. His wife, ready with food; the hours in front of the television; the telephone call to his daughter in Germany; the sleep; the snoring; the farting on the bed: he knows the routine and he will do it again tomorrow.

The Man's Eyes

THESE EYES HAVE seen too much. They have seen the whole world. They have seen the very good and the very bad. They have seen the happiest of days and the saddest of days. These eyes don't want to open some days; they want to stay tight closed, scrunched up, afraid of what they might see. These eyes remember things they want to forget. They remember looking into the eyes of liars, those who knew the truth but wouldn't say. They remember looking into the eyes of those who hated for no reason, just because they were who they were. These eyes have seen things they never wanted to see. They have inspected wounds and pain. These eyes have looked with love, deep into the eyes of those they cherish and these eyes have wished that they could make it all go away with a look, a tear, a kindly glance.

Some days these eyes are alert, wide open, ready to take in the miracles that are blooming all around them. They want to see the brightest of flowers beaming into the world. They want to see ordinary things: the folding of tea-towels, the sweeping of rooms, the shy look of a child waking up. These eyes have seen recovery. They have seen buildings spring up and fences repaired and handshakes and hard work and kindness. These eyes have cried over unconditional love. These eyes have watched babies born and marriages and flourishing lives. These eyes have watched birds, set free, released into the wide world.

These yes.
These crinkled, kind, wise, old eyes.
These eyes have seen the whole world.

The Man in the Snow

YOU ARE IN your taxi, heading to the airport. Tired but still entranced with this beautiful country. It is starting to snow, just slightly, like the hesitant onset of love.

You've been cold the whole time you've been here. Why didn't you bring gloves and a scarf with you? The whole time, concentrating on your Albanian, with one part of your mind trying not to think about the chill in your fingers.

You're at a standstill at the corner of a street and you're hoping that it won't fall too thick or too quickly for you to make it. You've got an interview in Cornwall tomorrow and you absolutely must make it. And there's the flat to tidy before your Mum comes at the weekend, and you promised to make those cards for Emily. And the meal out on Friday. And the decision about whether to invite Matt to that weekend away. Or should you just leave it? Will he even care, anyway?

You look out to the street and there's a man, just standing there. He's wearing those light brown nylon trousers that look ever so smart but ever so cheap. The snow's falling more heavily now and it interrupts your staring. You're trying to read the sign he's holding up. A battered sign, on brown corrugated cardboard, with capital letters scrawled out in marker pen. Maybe it's a name? And there's a word scribbled on the sign: *Spital*. You know that word. You've definitely seen it before.

He looks so cold. He's got a jacket on, but it isn't thick.

Again, it is nylon and underneath he's wearing a shirt and tie. He stands, statue-like, holding his sign with resolution. He doesn't look like a beggar but he's definitely asking for something and you look around you for something to give.

You bought bread from the market this morning and it's all you have. Not even a few euros – you've already paid the taxi driver and you've nothing left. You lean forward and ask the taxi driver to give the bread to this man. 'No,' he is saying. 'No, no. Not bread for this man.'

Why is he being so mean? This man looks cold. Dignified but cold. And he definitely wants something. You've become obsessed with staring at this man and now you pray silently that the traffic won't move until you've managed to do something for him.

You move over to the other side of the taxi and start to undo the window. The taxi driver is shouting but you don't care now. He's in a frenzy but you feel it is your duty to at least connect with this man, this frozen creature alone in the snow.

You pass the man the bread. '*Faleminderit*,' he says. He takes the bread, nods his head, smiles a little smile at you, but you can see that his eyes are full of sadness. He doesn't want bread. You see this now and realise that you've probably made things worse.

You're glad to shut the window and put a pane of glass between you and the pain outside. The taxi driver is very cross and you can see that the man outside notices. As the conversation between you and the taxi driver becomes more animated, so the man gets nearer. The taxi driver is explaining to you that the man is trying to get money for a friend who needs surgery at a local hospital. You realise, suddenly, that your bread was an insult and a gift that would help in no way at all. *Shit*, you think, *I should have listened.*

The man approaches, distress and worry on his face. You open your window again and the man gets closer and reaches out to you. 'Not hurt you,' he says, 'I don't hurt you,' in that powerful, deep Albanian accent.

'I know,' you say to him, 'I know you won't hurt me. I'm not afraid of you. I'm sorry, I'm so sorry I didn't help you.'

The taxi pulls away as you stare at this man, no gloves, no scarf, bearing the cold and the indignity, all for friendship's sake.

How to Be a Kosovan Wedding Guest

T HE RETURNED GIRL puts on the attire of a wedding
guest. After all, it is her brother's wedding, it is the least
she can do. She paints her face: not too much, but just a brush
of red on the lips and a shiny dust under her eyebrows and
a whisper of drama at the corner of her eyes. And she wears
a dress that skims her and makes her feel aware of her body
and its power over the boy who will meet her father for the
first time today. She does not want to look like the others. She
doesn't want their pasted faces and their uncomfortable shoes
and their unmoving smiles.

She is happy for her brother, as happy as she can be, for
he is going to have a new life and his wife is excited about
her new life too. And she is glad of this. She is glad that they
share this joy. She hugs her new sister-in-law on the way. She
is looking forward to the evening and she is nervously alert
about what she has sent in the post today. Who knows what
it will bring? Who knows what it will bring?

And then there's the Kosovan Wife, getting ready for a
neighbour's wedding, wearing something long and flowing.
She wears tall, bold, upright shoes. She dabs a white powder
on her face. She smooths a cream into her trembling legs. She
is being taken to the wedding by her brother so that they can
hide the suitcase in the boot of the car. She makes an excuse
for this and says that she needs to drop in to see her mother
first, to talk about the present, or some other such thing. She

has a thickly painted face by now, but this does not hide the purposeful brow and the sorrowful look.

And the wedding is so full of people and they glide and they greet and they smile. The colourful dresses and the bright orange drinks and the gold of the tables and the chairs and the shimmering fabrics make the room glow. And the greetings between families and compliments and heartfelt wishes and the shrieking of the children make the room buzz. And the warmth of breath mingling, fingers touching, lips brushing cheeks, hands gripping and bodies dancing make the room swell.

The men shoot bullets, high, into the air, to signal the start of the couple's new life together. This celebratory firing into the heavens shows everyone that this couple are free to marry if they so wish. And they will carry on. And they will shoot. And they will people the earth if they so desire. And they will shoot if they really want to. And they will live their lives.

And they are sat at long tables and they drink the fizzy drinks that send bubbles up their noses and the Returned Girl, the sister of the groom, she looks around and sees her cousins and their husbands and their children and there is a sort of ache in her, there is a sort of ache. And she sees a young woman that she knew at school, although she was a year below: the Kosovan Wife. And there she is with her husband, such a dark, handsome man, and her two little children, a boy and girl and the Returned Girl looks at her and thinks she looks so beautiful, so motherly. *And there is a pang within her. And there is a pang within her.*

And when these two young women are dancing they end up next to each other, holding each other's hands whilst remaining nonchalant and rhythmical. And they move around the floor together, twisting this way and that, but always keeping with the beat, holding hands, lifting arms into small arches, linking families, neighbours, communities, friends. The Returned Girl feels a sort of nostalgia for this traditional life, and she feels she has sort of separated herself from this, in the city with the friends and the boyfriend and the writing and the university. And *she feels a sort of longing. And she feels a sort of longing.*

And as they move around to the Albanian beat, the other woman, the Kosovan Wife, wonders if this is, after all, all there is. She decides yes, then no, then yes, then no, with every footstep. She feels a sort of anger at the music. *It is always the same,* she thinks. And she smiles at the woman next to her, the Returned Girl, a girl she recognises from school. She thinks she is the sister of the groom. *Look at her, all modern,* she thinks. *I heard she went to live in the city,* she thinks. *And she feels a sort of longing. And she feels a sort of longing.*

And there is more dancing. And there is talking and laughter. And the girl with the children, the Kosovan Wife, holds them close as they stumble, drunk on Fanta and the late night, into sleep at the end of this exciting party. And she keeps them both on her lap and cuddles them close. *Like little hot bricks,* she thinks.

And the Returned Girl talks to her brother and she nestles close to her father's chest when they talk about her mother and how she would have liked to have been here. And they have placed a photograph of her on a table and she stares at her mother's image. And a woman comes over and speaks to her and says that she is a woman who knew her mother in the hills in the war and she says, 'You must be her daughter.'

And she replies, 'Yes I am.' And she musters up her voice

from deep inside her throat. 'I am Liridona,' she says, 'and I am a writer.'

And at another table the Kosovan Wife, the woman with two little children curled on her golden lap, is tapped on the shoulder by you and you say, 'Lulezime, are you ready to go?' And she looks a little lost for a moment and then she gets up and you take her to your car, into the darkness, into the future.

The Maiden in the Box

THE KING LEFT the room and when she came back she was dressed in a woman's clothes and all the men around her were amazed. She wore a long green and silver dress embroidered with tiny jewels and the men did not know if she was a woman or a spirit. She shimmered and shone and radiated power and wisdom and glory. Of course, her father's officials immediately recognised her as the king's daughter and they wept with joy that she had been found. They knew that they had been right in trusting the oldest and wisest advisor. 'Thank God you are safe,' they said, 'and you are such a valiant leader, so strong and powerful. The perfect king and now the perfect queen.'

'And now it is time for me to pass judgement,' she said, with a look of strength in her jaw.

The first thing she did was to pardon the tradesman but she told him to leave her kingdom and never to come back. 'If you come here again,' she said, 'I will not be so merciful.'

Then she gave money to the fishermen and she told the man with the horse to leave. 'I see that poverty and loneliness drove you to wickedness,' she said. 'See that it does not do this to you again. You must always choose to do good, no matter what your fortunes may be.'

And then she turned to her husband. He looked so old and young and sad and happy and innocent and guilty. She stared at him and looked deep into his eyes. She looked at his trembling hands, she noticed his ashen face, she felt his contrite heart. He fell to his knees and he begged for her forgiveness. 'I have caused you great harm,' he said, 'I did not value you as I should have done. Believe me, I am truly sorry.'

She told him to rise and to sit at her side. He was made a prince, with her as Queen of Egypt, and the royal advisors announced to everyone in the land that the king's daughter had been found, that she had indeed been their king all along. There was much joy in the land. The feasting and rejoicing lasted for days.

The Children

THESE CHILDREN ARE beautiful. Eager to try, eager to learn, eager to be competitive, eager to shout, eager to be silent, eager to lead, eager to follow. Eager to love.

They play in a park at the edge of the town. The back edge, behind the dust and the bricks and the wood and the hospital. Behind the bartering, the buying, the selling, the boredom. Behind the learning, the numbing, the hoping, the heartbreak. Behind the romance and the infidelity and the daily lives and the dreams. Behind the frustrated, the excited, the bored, the lonely, the loved, the rememberers, the forgetters. Those here and now, those gone and past.

Who can say what's happened on this land before this moment? We know some of it. We know vulgarity, we know occupation, we know fear, we know murder and not just from the outsiders. We know that everyone doesn't love. We've learnt it, of course.

But now, just now, this piece of land is sacred. Prayed for by the believers, all kinds; hoped and wished for by the unbelievers: this piece of land is dedicated to good, to peace, to healing.

There are two little boys, blue jackets, the most enormous smiles on their faces. They laugh at everything. Funny or not, life is one big joke for these two. They hear the strange English people talking in the park and it is just hilarious. So funny, so ridiculous is their language. They can't suppress their giggles.

They have come here with a purpose. There is a long, grey slope through the middle of this land and they have come on their rollerskates, ready for a thrill. They drag each other up the slope, slipping at times and sometimes falling over. But remember, everything is funny to these two. Cuts and scrapes are laughable, part of the adventure.

At the top of the hill they spy their way down. The town is in the distance and they haven't even seen it. All they can register is this long, snaking slope and the intense pleasure they will feel on the way down. They breathe in the air, they laugh again, chattering away as they prepare themselves for the fun.

A streak of blue shoots down the slope and a cry of joy, as alive as a newborn baby, fills the air. 'Wooooooooooooooooh!' he cries. 'Wooo! Woo! Wooooooooooooooooooooooooo!'

He stops himself by lurching himself onto the grass. He falls over, but he is laughing, laughing, laughing, laughing, laughing.

And his friend, waiting at the top, shouts something loud and vital at him. Again, they both laugh, with that raucous sound.

His friend, the second blue bolt of speed, has his moment of abandon. A cobalt bird flying in the wind. 'Wooooooooooooooooooooooooooo!' He, more skilled, swoops his foot like a professional to stop his acceleration. The other boy comes up to him and wraps his arms around him.

They hug and smile and laugh again and push each other, as little boys often do. Their parents at home, they are free to enjoy their afternoon, to enjoy the speed, free of mother's carefuls and father's chiding eyes. They gesticulate and shout. They make silly faces and pretend to speak English, but it is all made up. This makes it even funnier.

No one in the world could help but love these two at this very moment. They are so full of joy.

Someone, somewhere, remembers these two and is glad that guns were silenced and tanks were turned back and hatred was not allowed its reign over this piece of land.

Acknowledgements

'THE MILK' WAS first published in the *Refugees and Peacekeepers* anthology by Patrician Press in January 2017. I also used Robert Elsie's translation work on www.albanianliterature.net to inspire 'The Maiden in the Box'.

Thanks, first and foremost, to Nick Royle for the encouragement to keep writing about Kosovo and for wanting to see my stories published. Many thanks also to Jen and Chris Hamilton-Emery for running the wonderful Salt Publishing and for agreeing to publish this novel. Thank you to Livi Michael for her very kind words.

Thank you to Rrezarta Mulolli, Fahrie Mulolli, Armend Bajgora, Nazmi Bajgora, Tahire Bajgora, Agron Bajgora, Fitim Topanica, Sanije Topanica, Ermina Topanica and Ardian Ibrahimi for sharing your stories with me. Thank you to Fazli Blakcori for telling me about Kosovan culture and for answering so many of my questions.

A huge thank you to Arja Suddens for letting me stay in her beautiful French house to write this.

Thank you to the MMU writers for all your encouragement, especially to the brilliant Eileen McAuley who has helped me in a million ways with my writing.

Thank you to Evita Jakupi, Erisa Maqani and Rina Ahmetaj for the Albanian guidance.

Thank you to my biological family who taught me that other people matter and who gave me the confidence to be creative. Particular thanks to my sisters, Chloe and Lauren Hamill, who kept me company at various times when I was writing.

Thank you to my MaK family for all your friendship. Special thanks to my dear friend, Pam Dawes.

Thank you to Stephen Raw for the perfect book cover. And for such a great mug.

Thank you to my friends Claire Millett, Kate Goddard, Maggie Carroll, Claire James and Natalie Harrison for reading, encouragement, cheerleading and corrections.

NEW BOOKS FROM SALT

XAN BROOKS
The Clocks in This House All Tell Different Times
(978-1-78463-093-5)

RON BUTLIN
Billionaires' Banquet (978-1-78463-100-0)

MICKEY J CORRIGAN
Project XX (978-1-78463-097-3)

MARIE GAMESON
The Giddy Career of Mr Gadd (deceased) (978-1-78463-118-5)

LESLEY GLAISTER
The Squeeze (978-1-78463-116-1)

NAOMI HAMILL
How To Be a Kosovan Bride (978-1-78463-095-9)

CHRISTINA JAMES
Fair of Face (978-1-78463-108-6)

SIMON KINCH
Two Sketches of Disjointed Happiness (978-1-78463-110-9)

This book has been typeset by
SALT PUBLISHING LIMITED
using Neacademia, a font designed by Sergei Egorov
for the Rosetta Type Foundry in the Czech Republic.
It is manufactured using Creamy 70gsm, a Forest
Stewardship Council™ certified paper from Stora Enso's
Anjala Mill in Finland. It was printed and bound by
Clays Limited in Bungay, Suffolk, Great Britain.

LONDON
GREAT BRITAIN
MMXVII